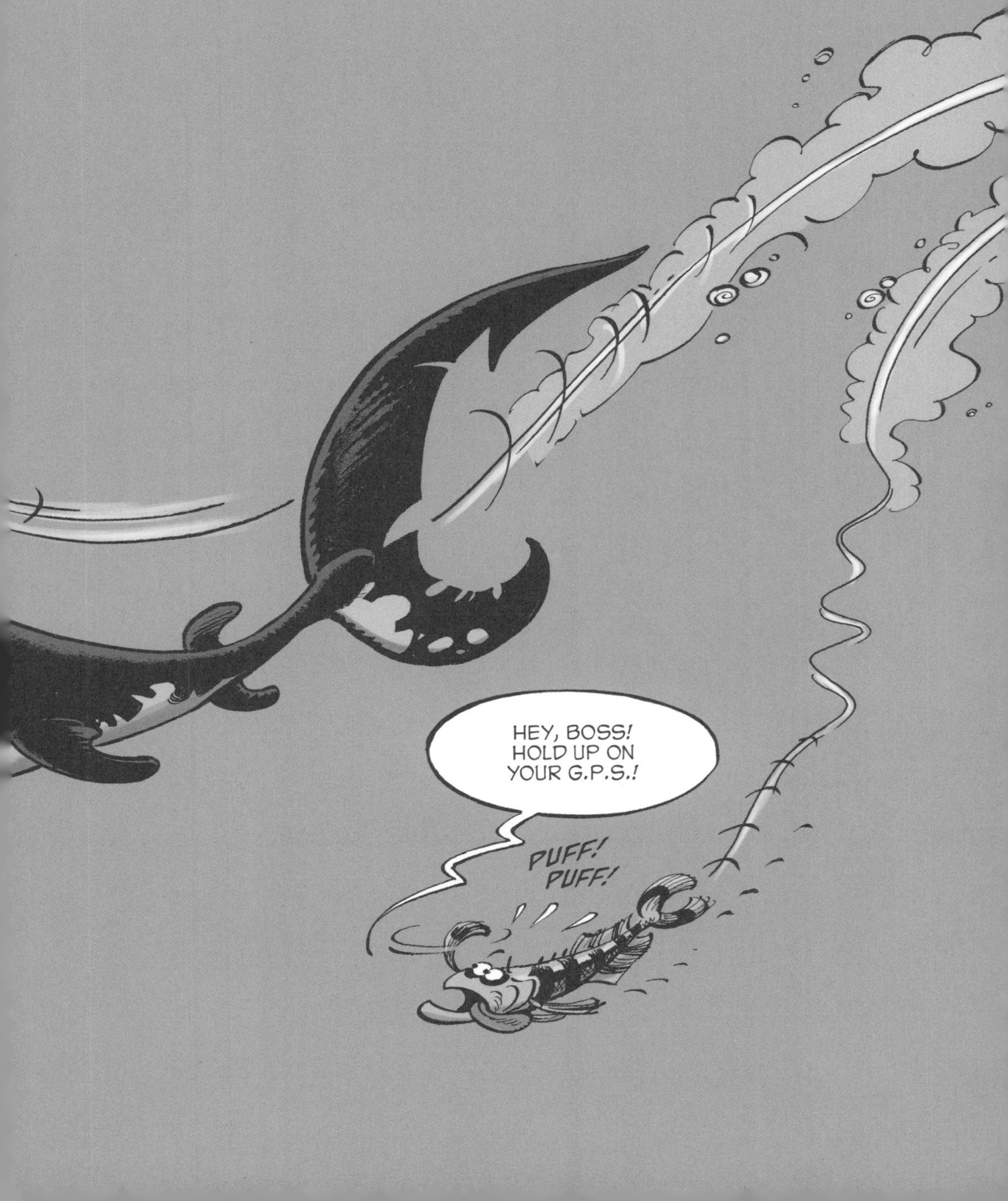
HEY, BOSS!
HOLD UP ON
YOUR G.P.S.!
PUFF!
PUFF!

in their own words

1. REEF MADNESS

Christophe Cazenove
Writer

Jytéry
Artist

Alexandre Amouriq & Mirabelle
Colorists

PAPERCUTZ
New York

THREATENED SPECIES RATINGS

Here are various statuses that the International Union for the Conservation of Nature (IUCN) assigns to species, which you'll find used about different sea creatures in these pages. The IUCN evaluates species using several criteria, such as population size, habitat destruction, number of individuals that have reached sexual maturity, etc.

NE: Not evaluated – no data to allow the species to be evaluated according to the criteria.
DD: Insufficient data – data does not allow for evaluation.
LC: Least concern – this is where we put species that have been evaluated but that don't go into the categories below. Humans fit in here.
NT: Near threatened – close to fulfilling all the criteria to become threatened in the near future.
VU: Vulnerable – facing an elevated risk of extinction in the wild.
EN: Threatened – Very high risk of extinction in the wild.
CR: Critically threatened – extremely high risk of extinction in the wild.
EW: Lost species that only exists in cultivation.
EX: Species has completely vanished.

A big thank you to Arnaud Plumeri for having had the idea of making educational cartoons, from which I've learned so many things.

-Christophe

Thank you to Christophe, for having put on his snorkel and mask in order to immerse us in these lovely fish tales…because he always finds us good jokes, even when he's holding his breath.

A special thank you to Alexandre and Mirabelle for their superb colors.

And thank you to Bamboo for being a real think tank.

-Jytéry

SEA CREATURES IN THEIR OWN WORDS
Les Animaux Marins en Bande Dessinee [Sea Creatures in Comics] by Cazenove and Jytéry © 2013 BAMBOO ÉDITION.
www.bamboo.fr
All other editorial material © 2017 by Papercutz.

**SEA CREATURES IN THEIR OWN WORDS #1
"REEF MADNESS"**
Christophe Cazenove – Writer
Thierry Jytéry – Artist
Alexandre Amouriq & Mirabelle – Colors
Nanette McGuinness – Translation
Janice Chiang – Letterer
JayJay Jackson – Additional Art
Big Bird Zatryb – Production
Mellisa Kleynowski– Editorial Intern
Sasha Kimiatek – Production Coordinator
Robert V. Conte – Editor
Jeff Whitman – Assistant Managing Editor
Jim Salicrup
Editor-in-Chief

ISBN: 978-1-62991-661-3

Printed in China
January 2017 by CP Printing LTD.

Distributed by Macmillan
First Papercutz Printing

THE OCTOPUS' LITTLE HABIT

THE OCTOPUS HAS A HABIT OF COLLECTING EVERYTHING IT FINDS...

WOW, A ROCK!

GREAT, A SHELL!

SCRATCH SCRATCH

AWESOME, A SODA CAN!

WHICH IT IMMEDIATELY PLACES IN FRONT OF THE ENTRANCE TO THE ROCK WHERE IT LIVES!

CAAAAREFULLY...! CAAAAAREFULLY...!

ON TENTACLE TIPS!

WHEN SOMETHING DANGEROUS APPROACHES, LIKE A CONGER EEL, FOR EXAMPLE...

≀RAAAH!≀ DANGER!

YIKES! I'M DEAD! QUICK! QUICK!

...IT COLLECTS THE ITEMS AT TOP SPEED...

SWOOSH

SWOOSH

SWOOSH

...TO BARRICADE ITSELF IN ITS SHELTER!

≀OOF!≀

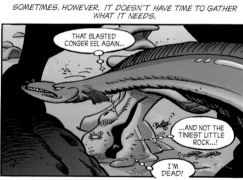

SOMETIMES, HOWEVER, IT DOESN'T HAVE TIME TO GATHER WHAT IT NEEDS.

THAT BLASTED CONGER EEL AGAIN...

...AND NOT THE TINIEST LITTLE ROCK...!

I'M DEAD!

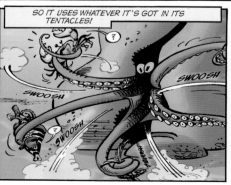

SO IT USES WHATEVER IT'S GOT IN ITS TENTACLES!

?

SWOOSH

SWOOSH

?

SWOOSH

BASED ON THAT, IT SHOULDN'T BE SURPRISING THAT THE OCTOPUS ISN'T VERY POPULAR WITH ITS NEIGHBORS!

HEY-HO! NOPE, THAT WON'T FIT!

≀GRRR!≀

WHAT KIND OF MANNERS ARE THESE?!

FLATFISH

DADDY, IS IT NORMAL FOR THEM TO BE TOTALLY FLAT?

WELL YEAH, BUT IT DOESN'T HAPPEN WITH THE FLIP OF A FIN!

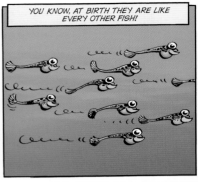

YOU KNOW, AT BIRTH THEY ARE LIKE EVERY OTHER FISH!

THEY START TO CHANGE BETWEEN 5 AND 120 MILLIMETERS*, THEN THEY SETTLE DOWN ON THE OCEAN FLOOR.

DON'T WAIT FOR ME, GUYS! I'M GOING TO SETTLE IN HERE. IT'S A REALLY GREAT SPOT!

*.2 TO 5 INCHES

"ONE OF THEIR EYES MIGRATES ONTO THE SAME SIDE AS THE OTHER..."

IT LOOKS LIKE A PICASSO!

AND BINGO!

ARRH! THAT MUST HURT A WHOLE LOT!

HA! HA! HA!

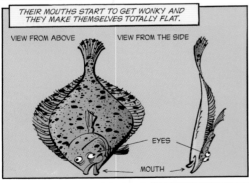

THEIR MOUTHS START TO GET WONKY AND THEY MAKE THEMSELVES TOTALLY FLAT.

VIEW FROM ABOVE

VIEW FROM THE SIDE

EYES

MOUTH

THERE ARE LOTS OF SPECIES THAT CHANGE LIKE THIS...THE SOLE, THE TURBOT--

AND THE GROUPER, TOO!

AH, NO, NOT THE GROUPER...

...IT CHANGED BECAUSE I SAT DOWN ON HIM BY ACCIDENT!

GULP!

THE INCREDIBLE STARFISH

AH, SO I SEE YOU ARE INTERESTED IN THE STARFISH, TOO?

THERE ARE AROUND 1,600 SPECIES OF THIS AMAZING CREATURE! DID YOU KNOW THAT?

IF YOU CUT OFF ONE OF ITS ARMS, ⸼POOF!⸼ IT GROWS BACK! WELL, NOT THE NEXT MINUTE, BUT STILL!

"AND IF ITS FOOD IS TOO BIG FOR ITS MOUTH, DO YOU KNOW WHAT IT DOES?

DRAT! THAT WILL NEVER FIT!

CLACK CLACK CLACK

"IT BRINGS ITS OWN STOMACH OUT OF ITS BODY...

"...THAT STARTS DIGESTING ITS PREY ON THE SPOT!"

BLEURRARRRGLE

ZIP

FOR AN ANIMAL THAT HAS NEITHER HEAD NOR BRAIN, IT IS TOTALLY FASCINATING!

PLUS IT'S FOR GAMES!

GAMES? THE STARFISH? I DIDN'T KNOW THAT!

WITHOUT IT, WE'D REALLY GET BORED ON WEEKENDS!

???

4 TO 2! FOR NOW!

THE SIZE OF FISH

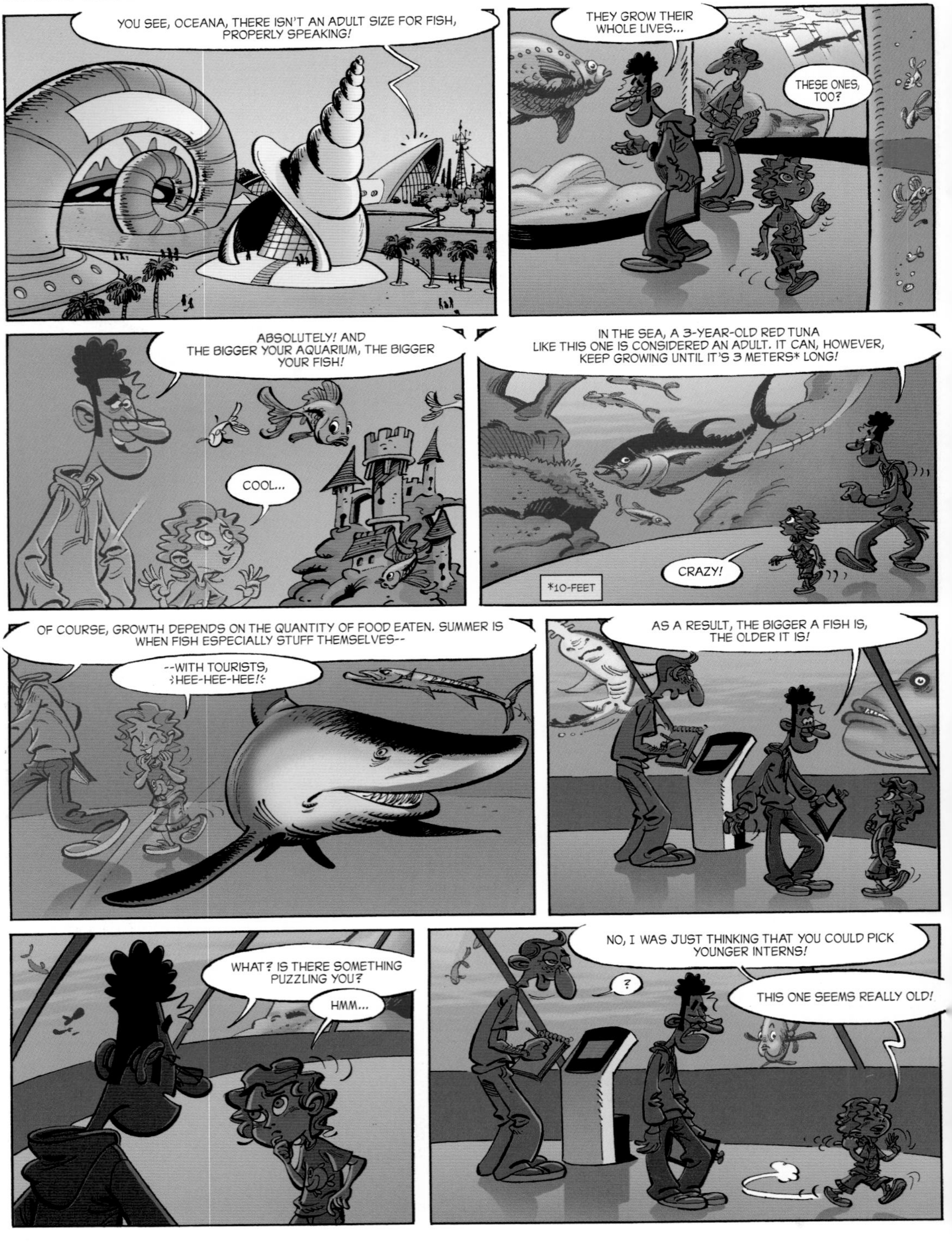

YOU SEE, OCEANA, THERE ISN'T AN ADULT SIZE FOR FISH, PROPERLY SPEAKING!
THEY GROW THEIR WHOLE LIVES...
THESE ONES, TOO?
ABSOLUTELY! AND THE BIGGER YOUR AQUARIUM, THE BIGGER YOUR FISH!
COOL...
IN THE SEA, A 3-YEAR-OLD RED TUNA LIKE THIS ONE IS CONSIDERED AN ADULT. IT CAN, HOWEVER, KEEP GROWING UNTIL IT'S 3 METERS* LONG!
CRAZY!
*10-FEET
OF COURSE, GROWTH DEPENDS ON THE QUANTITY OF FOOD EATEN. SUMMER IS WHEN FISH ESPECIALLY STUFF THEMSELVES--
--WITH TOURISTS, HEE-HEE-HEE!
AS A RESULT, THE BIGGER A FISH IS, THE OLDER IT IS!
WHAT? IS THERE SOMETHING PUZZLING YOU?
HMM...
NO, I WAS JUST THINKING THAT YOU COULD PICK YOUNGER INTERNS!
?
THIS ONE SEEMS REALLY OLD!

BUBBLE CURTAIN

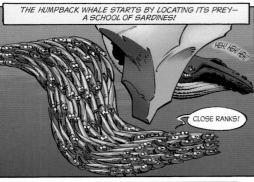

THE HUMPBACK WHALE STARTS BY LOCATING ITS PREY-- A SCHOOL OF SARDINES!

HEH! HEH! HEH!

CLOSE RANKS!

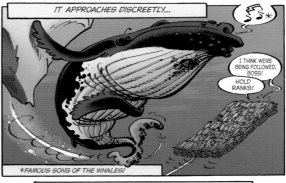

IT APPROACHES DISCREETLY...

I THINK WE'RE BEING FOLLOWED, BOSS!

HOLD RANKS!

*FAMOUS SONG OF THE WHALES!

THEN IT CIRCLES AROUND THEM, RELEASING A THICK CURTAIN OF BUBBLES...

? ? ? ? ? ? ? ?

HEH! HEH! HEH!

CONFUSED, ITS VICTIMS CAN'T ESCAPE!

WHERE ARE WE ALL?

WHAT A FOG!

CLOSE RANKS! CLO--

WHO'S TALKING?

THE WHALE RUSHES IN TO SWALLOW THOUSANDS OF THEM IN ONE FELL SWOOP!

YUM YUM

YUM YUM

SO YOU UNDERSTAND WHAT IT DOES?!

YUP!

BURP!

COME ON, GUYS, GET A MOVE ON! WE'LL MAKE OUR OWN CURTAIN OF BUBBLES, TOO!

THAT'LL TEACH HIM!

SSSSNORE

YUP, WE REALLY OWE THAT TO OUR BUDDIES!

FLOP FLOP

HUMPBACK WHALE
Megaptera novaeangliae

- **SIZE:** 15 meters [50 feet]
- **DIET:** Carnivore
- **DISTINCTIVE FEATURE:** At birth, the baby whale measures 4-5 meters long [13-16 feet] and weighs a ton. That's right, a big baby!

DEPTH: 0-180 METERS [590 FEET]	LC*	GEOGRAPHICAL LOCATION

*THREATENED SPECIES RATING. SEE THE TABLE ON PAGE TWO.

THE GREAT WHITE SHARK

YOU ALREADY KNOW THAT THE GREAT WHITE SHARK CAN SNIFF OUT A DROP OF BLOOD DILUTED IN WATER FROM MILES AWAY...

SNIFF SNIFF SNIFF...

A CUT ON A DIVER'S FINGER...

...3.75 MILES AWAY, NORTH TO NORTHEAST!

...BUT ITS HEARING IS VERY GOOD, TOO!

EEEEKKKK!
ARGH!! AIEEEEE!!
GLUB-GLUB

HEH! HEH! THAT'S A BOAT SINKING.

IT HAS EXCELLENT EYESIGHT...

YUM... SEALS!

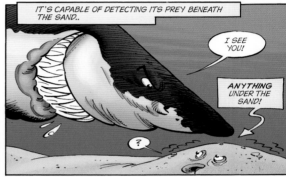

IT'S CAPABLE OF DETECTING ITS PREY BENEATH THE SAND..

I SEE YOU!

ANYTHING UNDER THE SAND!

?

IT SWIMS UP TO ALMOST 30 MILES PER HOUR!

ARF! ARF! ARF!

AND IF IT LOSES A TOOTH, ANOTHER AUTOMATICALLY GROWS BACK IN ITS PLACE!

SEE, IT GREW BACK IN! I DON'T LIKE CHEWING WITH ONE LESS TOOTH!

IN SHORT, IT'S A WEAPON OF WAR MADE FOR HUNTING KILLING, AND EATING!

HEY, BOSS! WHAT HAPPENED TO YOU?

WEREN'T YOU LISTENING?! WITH ALL MY FRIENDS PROWLING IN THE NEIGHBORHOOD, IT'S SUPER DANGEROUS AROUND HERE!

8

WHEN THE MONKFISH HUNTS...

THE MONKFISH SPENDS ITS DAYS HUNTING, HALF-BURIED IN THE MUD...

SHAKE SHAKE

TO DO THIS, IT SHAKES A THREAD ATTACHED TO ITS HEAD, IN ORDER TO ATTRACT GREEDY LITTLE FISH...

WOW! THAT LOOKS REALLY GOOD!

SHAKE SHAKE

...WHICH IT SWALLOWS UP IN ONE GULP!

SNAP

THEN IT STARTS SHAKING ITS LURE AGAIN...

SHAKE SHAKE

AGAIN...

SHAKE SHAKE

AND AGAIN...

SHAKE... SHAKE...

YES, WELL, THE MONKFISH IS HAPPY TO HEAD HOME IN THE EVENING...

SHAKE SHAKE... SHAKE...

WIPED OUT...

HOME SWEET HOME

I FEEL CRANKY! THE LITTLE ONE'S BEEN CRYING SINCE THIS MORNING AND I COULDN'T CALM HIM! YOU TAKE CARE OF HIM!

WA-AWAAAAHH

SHAKE SHAKE

WEE - SNIFF-SNIFF! HEE-HEE! HEE-HEE!

GOO?

COMMON MONKFISH
Lophius piscatorius

- SIZE: Up to 2 meters [6 feet]
- DIET: Carnivore
- DISTINCTIVE FEATURE: The head of the monkfish makes up roughly 50% of its total weight. It's quite a maw!

DEPTH: 0-1000 METERS [0-3300 FEET]	NT*	GEOGRAPHICAL LOCATION

*THREATENED SPECIES RATING. SEE THE TABLE ON PAGE TWO.

PEARL OYSTER

HOW DO OYSTERS MAKE PEARLS? THAT'S A GOOD QUESTION ISN'T IT?

"FOR THAT TO HAPPEN, A FOREIGN OBJECT HAS TO ENTER THE SHELL. FOR EXAMPLE...

HELLO THERE, DUMMY!

?

"TO HELP REDUCE THE IRRITATION THE INTRUDER CAUSES, THE OYSTER REACTS BY COATING IT WITH MOTHER OF PEARL...

HOLY COW! THAT REALLY ITCHES!

SCRATCH SCRATCH...

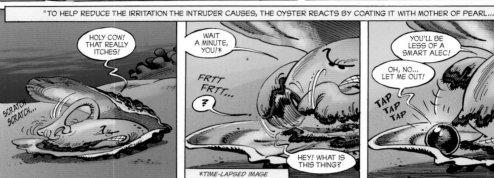

WAIT A MINUTE, YOU!*

FRTT FRTT...

?

HEY! WHAT IS THIS THING?

*TIME-LAPSED IMAGE

YOU'LL BE LESS OF A SMART ALEC!

OH, NO... LET ME OUT!

TAP TAP TAP

OVER THE YEARS, THESE MOTHER-OF-PEARL DEPOSITS FORM A MAGNIFICENT PEARL!

"THIS IS THE TECHNIQUE THAT PEARL CULTIVATORS USE, DEPOSITING A FOREIGN OBJECT-- THE 'NUCLEON'--INTO THE OYSTER."

AND SO...

ARE YOU SURE THAT YOU'LL GET THE BIGGEST PEARLS DOING IT THIS WAY?

SEEMS LOGICAL, DOESN'T IT? PASS ME ANOTHER BALL...

SEA MONSTERS

MILLIONS OF YEARS AGO, THE OCEANS HARBORED TERRIFYING CREATURES!

"LIKE THE **MEGALODON**, A PREDATOR WITH A JAW 2 METERS (6.5 FEET) BIG, FILLED WITH TEETH OVER 20 CENTIMETERS (8 INCHES) LARGE!

"THE **XIPHACTINUS**, A KIND OF GIANT PIRANHA...

"THE **DUNKLEOSTEUS**, A 5-TON ARMORED FISH...

"THE **BASILOSAURUS**, THE LARGEST CETACEAN KNOWN, CAPABLE OF REACHING 25 METERS (82 FEET) IN SIZE!

"AND ALSO THE **ELASMOSAURUS**...

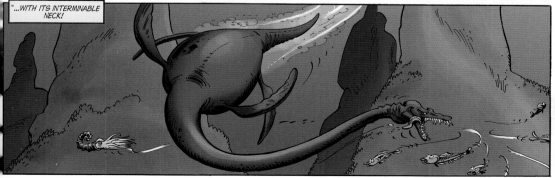

"...WITH ITS INTERMINABLE NECK!

"WE COULD ALSO COME ACROSS THE SCORPION OF THE SEA, THE *PTERYGOTUS*...

"THE *TYLOSAURUS*, A MARINE LIZARD...

"THE *LEEDICTHYS*, THE BIGGEST FISH EVER DISCOVERED, 15 METERS (50 FEET)...

"THE *LIOPLEURODON*, WITH ITS SMOOTH-SIDED TEETH!

"...AND MANY OTHERS, ALL JUST AS TERRIFYING!"

LUCKILY, TODAY ALL THESE MARINE MONSTERS HAVE DISAPPEARED!

NOT SO BAD!

I WOULDN'T LIKE TO COME ACROSS ONE OF THEM!

IT'S TRUE THAT THEY KNEW WHO THEY LIKED, HA! HA! HA!

WHAT?

WHAT DID I SAY?

CAR WASH

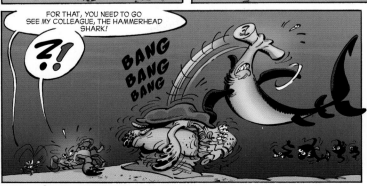

CLEANER SHRIMP
Stenopus Hispidus

- **SIZE:** 7-10 centimeters [3-4 inches]
- **DIET:** Detritivore, Detritophage
- **DISTINCTIVE FEATURE:** Surprisingly enough, the dirtier the fish, the more it will love it.

DEPTH: 0-15 METERS [0-50 FEET]	NE*	GEOGRAPHICAL LOCATION

*THREATENED SPECIES RATING. SEE THE TABLE ON PAGE TWO.

THREATENED SPECIES

THERE ARE MANY THREATENED SPECIES IN THE MARINE WORLD...

?!!

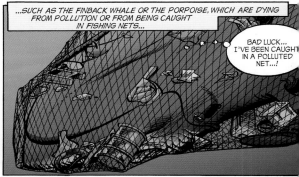

...SUCH AS THE FINBACK WHALE OR THE PORPOISE, WHICH ARE DYING FROM POLLUTION OR FROM BEING CAUGHT IN FISHING NETS...

BAD LUCK... I'VE BEEN CAUGHT IN A POLLUTED NET...!

THE SEAL IS A VICTIM OF A REAL MASSACRE!

TACKATACKTACKA...

PFTT

PFTT

OVERFISHING HAS THREATENED THE EEL...

...THE RED TUNA...

SUSHI BAR

WELL, WHAT DO YOU KNOW. YOU GOT NABBED, TOO?

OH, YEAH!

...AND THE COD!

¡CLACK¡
¡CLACK¡
¡CLACK¡
¡CLACK¡

I KNOW HOW YOU FEEL--I'M THREATENED, TOO!

?

TOOT TOOT

YOU? DON'T MAKE ME LAUGH! SINCE WHEN HAVE SARDINES BEEN IN DANGER OF GOING EXTINCT?

TOOT TOOT

ME? EVERY EVENING!

STILL HANGING OUT UNTIL ALL HOURS OF THE NIGHT!

IF YOU DON'T COME COME RIGHT NOW, SPARKS WILL FLY! YOU GOOD FOR NOTHING!

PFFFF...

SLEEPING WITH THE FISHES

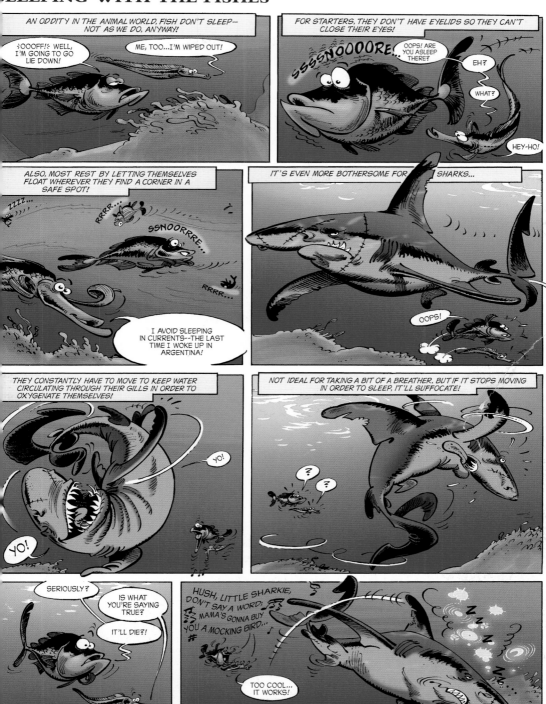

LIFE OUT OF WATER

A REAL, SELF-RESPECTING FISH LIVES UNDERWATER. WE'RE IN TOTAL AGREEMENT WITH THAT!

YOU BET!

WE'RE NOT SUICIDAL!

HOWEVER, SOME FISH DON'T HESITATE TO STICK THEIR NOSES OUT IN THE OPEN AIR...AND NOT JUST THEIR NOSES!

?

HUH? WHAT IS HE UP TO?

LIKE THE EEL WHEN IT'S LOOKING FOR ANOTHER BODY OF WATER...

?!

I HOPE MY GPS WON'T MESS ME UP!

THE *PERIOPHTALMUS MODESTUS*, WHICH LIES ON THE BRANCHES OF THE MANGROVE TREE...

A BIT OF SUNBATHING WITH YOUR HAREM DOES YOU SOME GOOD!

THE *KILLIFISH*, WHICH CAN SURVIVE SEVERAL WEEKS OUT OF WATER IN THE MANGROVE...

I'M THIRSTY!

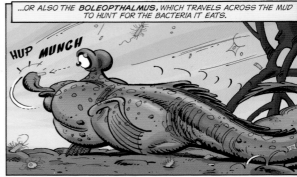

...OR ALSO THE *BOLEOPTHALMUS*, WHICH TRAVELS ACROSS THE MUD TO HUNT FOR THE BACTERIA IT EATS.

HUP MUNCH

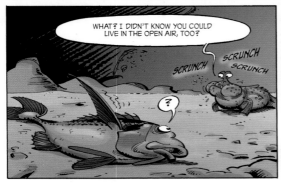

WHAT? I DIDN'T KNOW YOU COULD LIVE IN THE OPEN AIR, TOO?

SCRUNCH SCRUNCH SCRUNCH

?

N...NO! I WAS FOOLED BY THE TIDE! WHAT A DUMMY!

FLOP

FLIP FLOP

ARGH!

SCRUNCH SCRUNCH

THE TORPEDO RAY

NO--ARE YOU OUT OF YOUR MIND?

NOT AT ALL! WE TORPEDO RAYS HAVE TWO ELECTRIC ORGANS IN THE FRONT, ON EACH SIDE OF OUR HEADS.

AS A RESULT, I CAN DELIVER CHARGES FROM 40-220 VOLTS.*

DO YOU WANT ME TO SHOW YOU?

HMM...

*LIKE A LIGHT BULB.

ZWACK

WHOA! DANG!

ZWACK

ZWACK

ZZZT

ZWACK

THAT ROCKS!

...AND CAN YOU DO THAT FOR A LONG TIME?

ZZZT

ZZZT

OH, WELL, NO...WHEN I DO IT TOO OFTEN, LIKE NOW... I HAVE TO WAIT UNTIL I RECHARGE MYSELF...

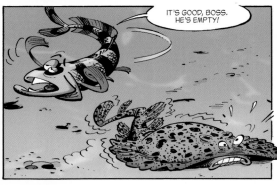

IT'S GOOD, BOSS. HE'S EMPTY!

I DON'T REALLY LIKE ELECTRICAL THINGUMMIES. I PREFER TRADITIONAL CUISINE!

BON APPÉTIT, BOSS!

TORPEDO RAY

Torpedo marmorata (translates to the Electric Ray)

- SIZE: 60-100 centimeters [25-40 inches]
- DIET: Carnivore
- DISTINCTIVE FEATURE: It burrows under the sand in order to hunt fish or shellfish and stun them with electrical shocks.

DEPTH: 0.5-200 METERS [2-650 FEET]	DD*	GEOGRAPHICAL LOCATION

*THREATENED SPECIES RATING. SEE THE TABLE ON PAGE TWO.

ON THE TRAIL OF THE PERIWINKLE

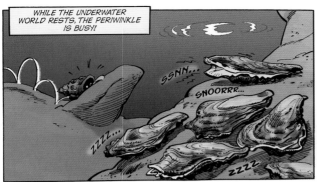

WHILE THE UNDERWATER WORLD RESTS, THE PERIWINKLE IS BUSY!

SSNN...

SNOORRR...

ZZZZ...

ZZZZ

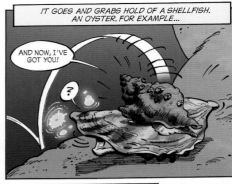

IT GOES AND GRABS HOLD OF A SHELLFISH. AN OYSTER, FOR EXAMPLE...

AND NOW, I'VE GOT YOU!

?

...WHICH IT PIERCES WITH ITS TONGUE, WHICH ACTS LIKE A DRILL...

CLANK

DZZZZZZ

?

IT DOES THIS TO GET TO THE FLESH AND EAT ITS PREY...

OUCH! I'M COOKED!

HEH! HEH! HEH! YUM-YUM!

ITS CRIME COMMITTED, IT TRIES TO FIND ANOTHER VICTIM...

BURP!

HOP

?

YUM-YUM!

ZZZZ

THEN ANOTHER AND ANOTHER...

DZZZ MUNCH MUNCH

DZZZ MUNCH MUNCH

DZZZ MUNCH MUNCH

MUNCH MUNCH MUNCH

THESE BURGLARIES HAVE A SIGNATURE! THE PERIWINKLE'S THE CULPRIT-- THE STUPIDEST OF ALL THE SHELLFISH!

WHY DO YOU SAY THAT, CHIEF?

IT TAKES EVERYTHING EXCEPT THE PEARLS!

THE ICEFISH

HOW COULD A FISH SURVIVE IN THE GLACIAL WATERS OF THE SOUTHERN OCEAN?

THE ICEFISH OR CROCODILE ICEFISH SEEM TO HAVE BECOME ADAPTED TO IT AS IT EVOLVED...

HOLY C-COW! I--IT'S REALLY FR-FREEZING...

CLACK CLACK CLACK

SO ITS BODY BEGAN TO PRODUCE ANTIFREEZE MOLECULES!

HAAA! WELL, THAT'S BETTER ALREADY, ALTHOUGH IT'S STILL NOT THE SAHARA EITHER!

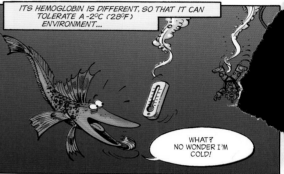

ITS HEMOGLOBIN IS DIFFERENT, SO THAT IT CAN TOLERATE A -2ºC (28ºF) ENVIRONMENT...

WHAT? NO WONDER I'M COLD!

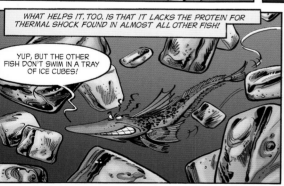

WHAT HELPS IT, TOO, IS THAT IT LACKS THE PROTEIN FOR THERMAL SHOCK FOUND IN ALMOST ALL OTHER FISH!

YUP, BUT THE OTHER FISH DON'T SWIM IN A TRAY OF ICE CUBES!

IT MAY NOT, HOWEVER, BE COMPLETELY FINISHED EVOLVING...

AH, NO, BUT THEN I'M REALLY FREEZING! I NEED TO ADAPT!

...AND HERE'S WHAT IT COULD LOOK LIKE!

AH...NO MATTER WHAT YOU SAY...

...EVOLUTION IS STILL GREAT...!

ICEFISH
Chionodraco hamatus

- **SIZE:** 50 centimeters [20 inches]
- **DIET:** Carnivore
- **DISTINCTIVE FEATURE:** What? The fact that it lives in freezing waters isn't enough for you?

DEPTH: 0-600 METERS [0-2000 FEET]	NE*	GEOGRAPHICAL LOCATION

*THREATENED SPECIES RATING. SEE THE TABLE ON PAGE TWO.

DOLPHIN SONAR

EVERYONE KNOWS THAT THE DOLPHIN IS A SPLENDID ANIMAL...

WELL... THAT'S YOUR OPINION...

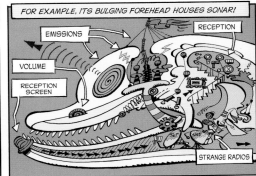

FOR EXAMPLE, ITS BULGING FOREHEAD HOUSES SONAR!

EMISSIONS

RECEPTION

VOLUME

RECEPTION SCREEN

STRANGE RADIOS

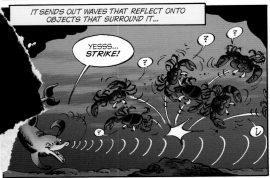

IT SENDS OUT WAVES THAT REFLECT ONTO OBJECTS THAT SURROUND IT...

YESSS... STRIKE!

...AND RETURN TO IT LIKE AN ECHO!

BONG

DANG! IT'S COMING BACK STRONGLY TODAY!

SO THE DOLPHIN HAS A VERY PRECISE IMAGE OF ITS ENVIRONMENT-- FISH, LANDSCAPE, PREDATORS, ETC.

NARRATION

SUBMARINE

PREDATOR

HORIZON

REAR VIEW

READER

EDGE OF THE FRAME...

FISH

UMM...TELL ME, IS YOUR SONAR PRECISE?

PRETTY SPOT ON. NOTHING ESCAPES ME!

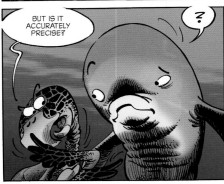

BUT IS IT ACCURATELY PRECISE?

?

IT'S NICE OF YOU TO HELP ME FIND THE KIDS!

IF MY WIFE FINDS OUT I LOST THEM, I'M GOING TO GET IT!

THE STURGEON'S JOURNEY

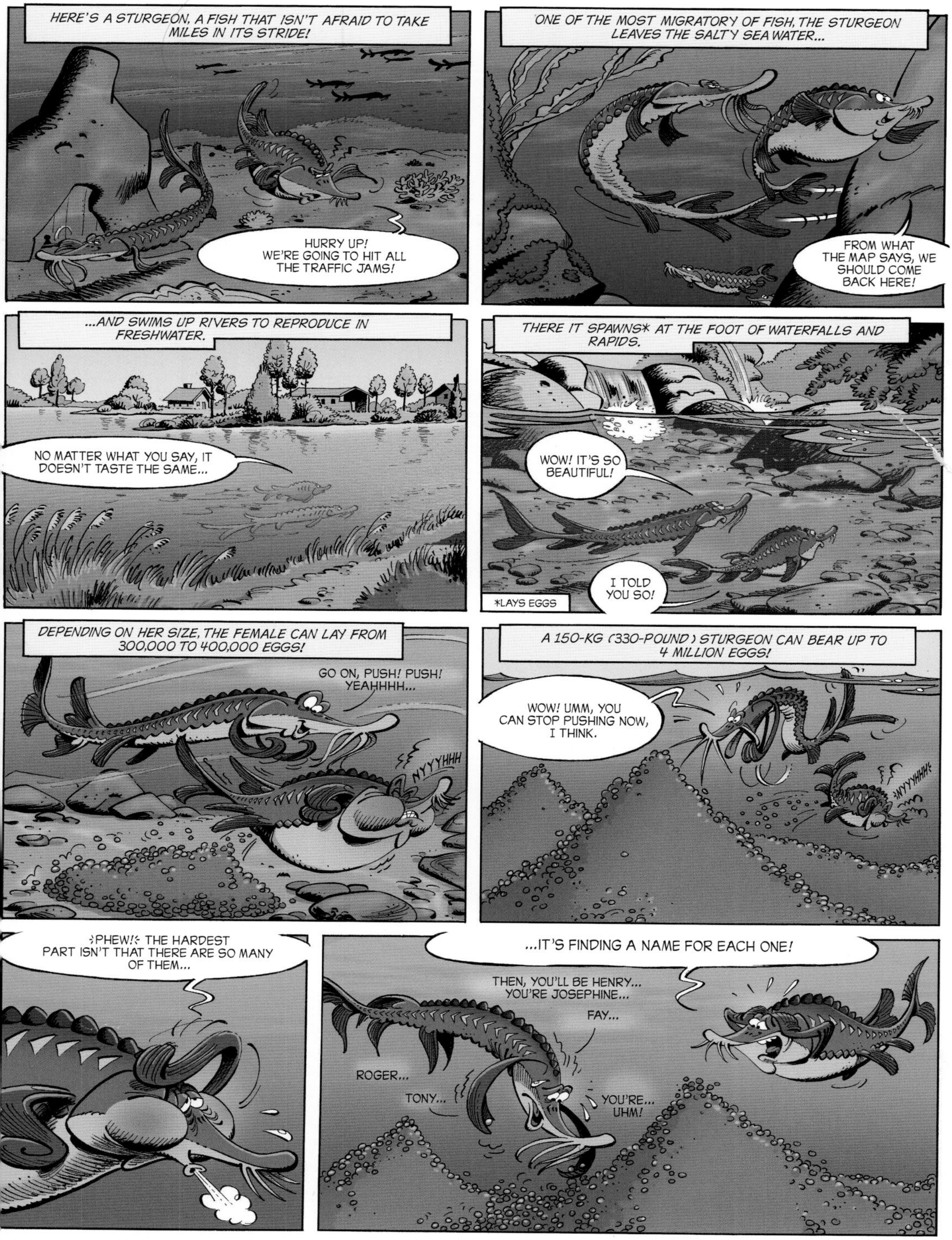

HERE'S A STURGEON, A FISH THAT ISN'T AFRAID TO TAKE MILES IN ITS STRIDE!
HURRY UP! WE'RE GOING TO HIT ALL THE TRAFFIC JAMS!
ONE OF THE MOST MIGRATORY OF FISH, THE STURGEON LEAVES THE SALTY SEA WATER...
FROM WHAT THE MAP SAYS, WE SHOULD COME BACK HERE!
...AND SWIMS UP RIVERS TO REPRODUCE IN FRESHWATER.
NO MATTER WHAT YOU SAY, IT DOESN'T TASTE THE SAME...
THERE IT SPAWNS* AT THE FOOT OF WATERFALLS AND RAPIDS.
WOW! IT'S SO BEAUTIFUL!
I TOLD YOU SO!
*LAYS EGGS
DEPENDING ON HER SIZE, THE FEMALE CAN LAY FROM 300,000 TO 400,000 EGGS!
GO ON, PUSH! PUSH! YEAHHHH...
NYYYHHH
A 150-KG (330-POUND) STURGEON CAN BEAR UP TO 4 MILLION EGGS!
WOW! UMM, YOU CAN STOP PUSHING NOW, I THINK.
NYYYHHH!
PHEW! THE HARDEST PART ISN'T THAT THERE ARE SO MANY OF THEM...
...IT'S FINDING A NAME FOR EACH ONE!
THEN, YOU'LL BE HENRY... YOU'RE JOSEPHINE...
FAY...
ROGER...
TONY...
YOU'RE... UHM!

A SCHOOL OF HERRING

A SCHOOL OF HERRING IS MADE UP OF HUNDREDS OF MILLIONS OF FISH THAT MOVE IN A SYNCHRONIZED FASHION...

ONE THOUGHT, ONE MOVEMENT...

DOWN!

TO THE LEFT!

UP!

THE CONNECTION BETWEEN EACH INDIVIDUAL MEMBER COMES INTO BEING WHEN THE DENSITY OF THE GROUP REACHES A CERTAIN LEVEL.

A LOAF OF OLIVE BREAD!

IN A BALL!

LIKE A SHARK!

ONE THOUGHT, ONE MOVEMENT...

YUM! IT'S FULL OF PLANKTON OVER THERE!

NOW'S THE MOMENT, AS THEY'RE ALL BUSY DOING WHATEVER...

DISCREETLY...

YUM! YUM!

HUP! ALL FOR YOURS TRULY!

YUM!

?

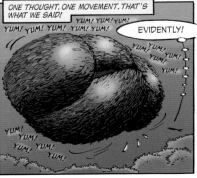

ONE THOUGHT, ONE MOVEMENT. THAT'S WHAT WE SAID!

YUM! YUM! YUM! YUM! YUM! YUM! YUM! YUM!
YUM! YUM! YUM! YUM! YUM!
YUM! YUM!
YUM! YUM! YUM! YUM! YUM!

EVIDENTLY!

HERRING
Culpea harengus

- **SIZE:** 40 centimeters [16 inches]
- **DIET:** Zooplankton
- **DISTINCTIVE FEATURE:** The schools form in the evening and disperse at sunrise. from that we can conclude that herring do not like to sleep alone.

DEPTH: 0-180 METERS [590 FEET]	LC*	GEOGRAPHICAL LOCATION

*THREATENED SPECIES RATING. SEE THE TABLE ON PAGE TWO.

HI!

UMM...DO YOU KNOW WHERE WE'RE SUPPOSED TO GO AROUND HERE?

WELL, WE JUST HAVE TO DO WHAT EVERYONE ELSE IS DOING. LOOK, THEY'RE ALL GOING TOWARDS THE SEA!

JEEPERS! THERE'RE A LOT OF THEM ON THE BEACH! HUNDREDS, AT LEAST!

THOUSANDS, I'M TELLING YOU!

WATCH OUT!

?

CLACK

CLACK

IS HE OUT OF HIS MIND?

OUCH!

KEEP UP THE PACE IF YOU CARE ABOUT YOUR SHELL!

ANOTHER CRAB?

SHRIEEEK SEAGULLS!

BUT WHAT DID WE DO TO THEM?!

I CAN'T BELIEVE IT! WE GOT THROUGH!

PLUNK

PLUNK

DO YOU KNOW THAT FEWER THAN 10 OUT OF 100,000 TURTLES SURVIVE THESE ATTACKS?

AND IT CAME DOWN TO US!

SO WE'RE WARRIORS! TRUE BEASTS!

NOTHING CAN STOP US!

SMAK

NOW WE CAN FACE CARNIVOROUS FISH, JACK FISH, TIGER SHARKS, WHITE SHARKS, BULL SHARKS...

YEAH! JUST YOU WAIT AND SEE! WE'RE GOING TO PUT THEM--

--GA-GLUB!

?

I'M GOING TO SHOW THEM WHO'S THE BOSS!

IT'LL BE AWESOME!

AS SOON AS I LEARN TO SWIM!

THE WORLD OF SILENCE

WE THINK THERE'S NO SOUND UNDER THE SEA—THAT IT'S A WORLD OF SILENCE—BUT THAT WOULD BE FORGETTING THE DOLPHIN'S WHISTLING...

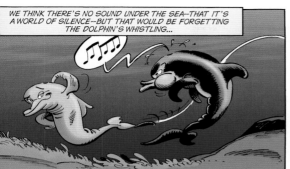

THE CATFISH CROAKING...

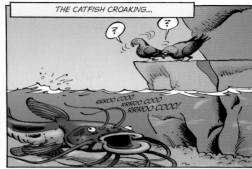

RRROO COOO
RRROO COOO
RRROO COOO!

THE CHATTERING OF COD, EELS, AND ROCKFISH...

BLAH BLAH
BLAH BLAH
BLAH BLAH

RATATI
RATATA
RATATUM

CHACH
CHACH
CHACH...

THE TOADFISH, WHICH PLAYS AT BEING AN OWL... THE SEA ROBIN'S GROWLING...

THEY BUG ME WITH THEIR "WHOO-WHOO!"

AND WHERE'S IT HIDING, FOR THAT MATTER?

THE CLOWNFISH, WHICH CLICKS ITS TEETH... THE MEAGER, WHICH RUMBLES...

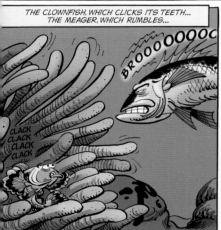

BROOOOOOOO

CLACK
CLACK
CLACK
CLACK

...OR ALSO THE AMAZING SONG OF THE WHALES!

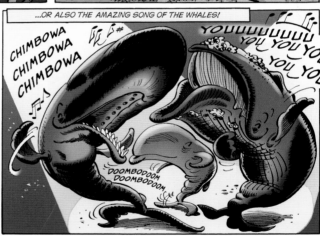

CHIMBOWA
CHIMBOWA
CHIMBOWA

YOUUUUUUU
YOU YOU YOU
YOU YOU

DOOMBODOOM
DOOMBODOOM

NO, I'D SAY...

IS THIS THE WORLD OF SILENCE HERE?!

CROOO COO
WHOO WHOO
CHIMBOWA
CHIMBOWA
CHIMBOWA
CLACK
CLACK
CLACK

BLAHBLAH
BLAH BLAHBLAH
DOOMBODOOM
DOOMBODOOM
EXCUSE ME?
RATATI
RATATA

GRRR
GRRRRR
BROOOO
YOOUUUUUU
YOU YOU YOU
CHICK
CHACK...
CHICK
CHACK...

THE PISTOL SHRIMP

BANG!

AH! WHAT'S THAT?

DON'T PANIC!

TAP-TAP TAP-TAP

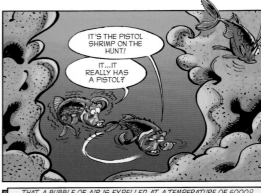

IT'S THE PISTOL SHRIMP ON THE HUNT!

IT...IT REALLY HAS A PISTOL?

NOOOO! THE THING IS, IT SNAPS ITS CLAW SO QUICKLY...

..THAT A BUBBLE OF AIR IS EXPELLED AT A TEMPERATURE OF 5000° AND MORE THAN 100 KM/HOUR (8000 DEGREES AND 60 MILES/HOUR)!

POW

WHEN IT EXPLODES, THE BUBBLE KNOCKS OUT ITS PREY!

BANG

AAAARRGH!

AND THAT'S WHAT MAKES THAT SOUND!

AH, OKAY... IT'S NOT A REAL PISTOL, THEN!

PFFFT

OH, MY... WHAT BAD LUCK!

??

SNIFF SNIFF SNIFF

IT WAS CLEANING ITS CLAW AND THE SHOT WENT OFF ON ITS OWN!

WHO'S AFRAID OF THE SHARK?

WOOF-WOOF-WOOF ARF-ARF-ARF

WHAT'S MAKING YOU GIGGLE LIKE THAT?

WE JUST SCARED THE LIVING DAYLIGHTS OUT OF SOME SWIMMERS!

ARF-ARF

WOOF-WOOF

OH, YEAH, I FORGET YOU'RE REAL TERRORS!

SHARKS KILL ABOUT 5 HUMANS A YEAR, RIGHT?

YUUPP

∻COUGH! COUGH!∻ JELLYFISH KILL AROUND A HUNDRED...

MOMMY!

AROUND 600 FOR ELEPHANTS...

POP

CRAAACK

SNAKES RACK UP A COUNT OF 100,000...

HEY! WOULD YOU STOP WAVING AROUND? I'D REALLY LIKE TO DIGEST IN PEACE!

...BETWEEN 40 AND 50 FOR DOGS...

RUFF-RUFF

HEEEELLPPP!

...WITH 150 DEATHS A YEAR, EVEN COCONUTS ARE MORE DANGER[OUS] THAN YOU ARE!

IT'S HARSH, WOULDN'T YOU SAY?

∻GULP!∻

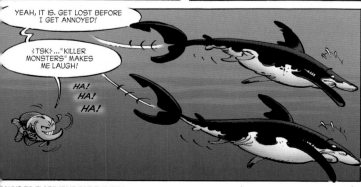

YEAH, IT IS. GET LOST BEFORE I GET ANNOYED!

∻TSK∻..."KILLER MONSTERS" MAKES ME LAUGH!

HA! HA! HA!

WHITE SHARK
Carcharodon carcharias

- **SIZE:** 6.5 meters [210 feet]
- **DIET:** Carnivore
- **DISTINCTIVE FEATURE:** Super precocious, the young can survive on their own as soon as they are born.

DEPTH: 0-1200 METERS [0-400 FEET]	VU*	GEOGRAPHICAL LOCATION

*THREATENED SPECIES RATING. SEE THE TABLE ON PAGE TWO.

THANKS TO FLORENTINE FOR THE IDEA.

THE LIMPET'S SUCTION EFFECT

THE LIMPET IS A SHELLFISH THAT HAS TO BE CAUGHT BY SURPRISE...

YUM!

BECAUSE AS SOON AS IT ATTACHES ITS SUCTION FOOT TO A ROCK...

RRRRR...

SHMOOB

...IT'S ALMOST IMPOSSIBLE TO PEEL IT OFF!

WAIT, I'LL GIVE YOU A HAND!

NYYYYHHH

PULL! JUST PULL!

THAT'S JUST WHAT I'M DOING!

FORGET IT! YOU'RE GOING TO CRACK A TOOTH!

YEAH! WE'VE BEEN AT THIS FORAGES!

AAAAARGHHHH!

HEE-HEE-HEE! THEY'RE NOT ABLE TO BREAK MY FOOT!

WELL, I'M GOING TO GO TEASE THEM A LITTLE BIT, HA-HA-HA!

? ? ?

HMMMM...

HELP! I'M STUUUUUCK!

HEH! HEH! HEH! HEH!

HEH! HEH!

LIMPET
Patella rustiqua

- **SIZE:** 5-7 centimeters [2-3 inches]
- **DIET:** Carnivore
- **DISTINCTIVE FEATURE:** Initially male, some lim[pets] become female; some of them return to being male lat[er]

DEPTH: 0-5 METERS [0-16 FEET]	NE*	GEOGRAPHIC LOCATION

*THREATENED SPECIES RATING. SEE THE TABLE ON PAGE TWO.

THE MYSTERY OF BEACHING

DO WE KNOW WHY THAT WHALE BEACHED ITSELF, DADDY?

UNFORTUNATELY NOT... MAYBE FATIGUE... BUT THEY'LL TAKE CARE OF IT AND PUT IT BACK INTO THE WATER, DON'T WORRY!

SOMETIMES AN ANIMAL THAT'S HUNTING GETS SURPRISED BY THE TIDE GOING OUT...

A STORM CAN ALSO CAUSE AN ANIMAL TO BECOME BEACHED...

?!

CETACEANS CAN GET DISORIENTED FROM MILITARY SHOOTING...

THAT'S REALLY STARTING TO MAKE A BIG RACKET!

?!

TAP TAP TAP

BUT THE MAJORITY OF BEACHING BY LIVING ANIMALS REMAINS A MYSTERY!

OTHERS, HOWEVER, CAN BE EXPLAINED VERY EASILY!

OH, YEAH? WHICH?

THOSE BY CERTAIN HUMAN BEINGS, PARTICULARLY!

99 BOTTLES OF BEER ON THE WALL... 99 BOTTLES OF BEER...

SPONGE

PILOT FISH

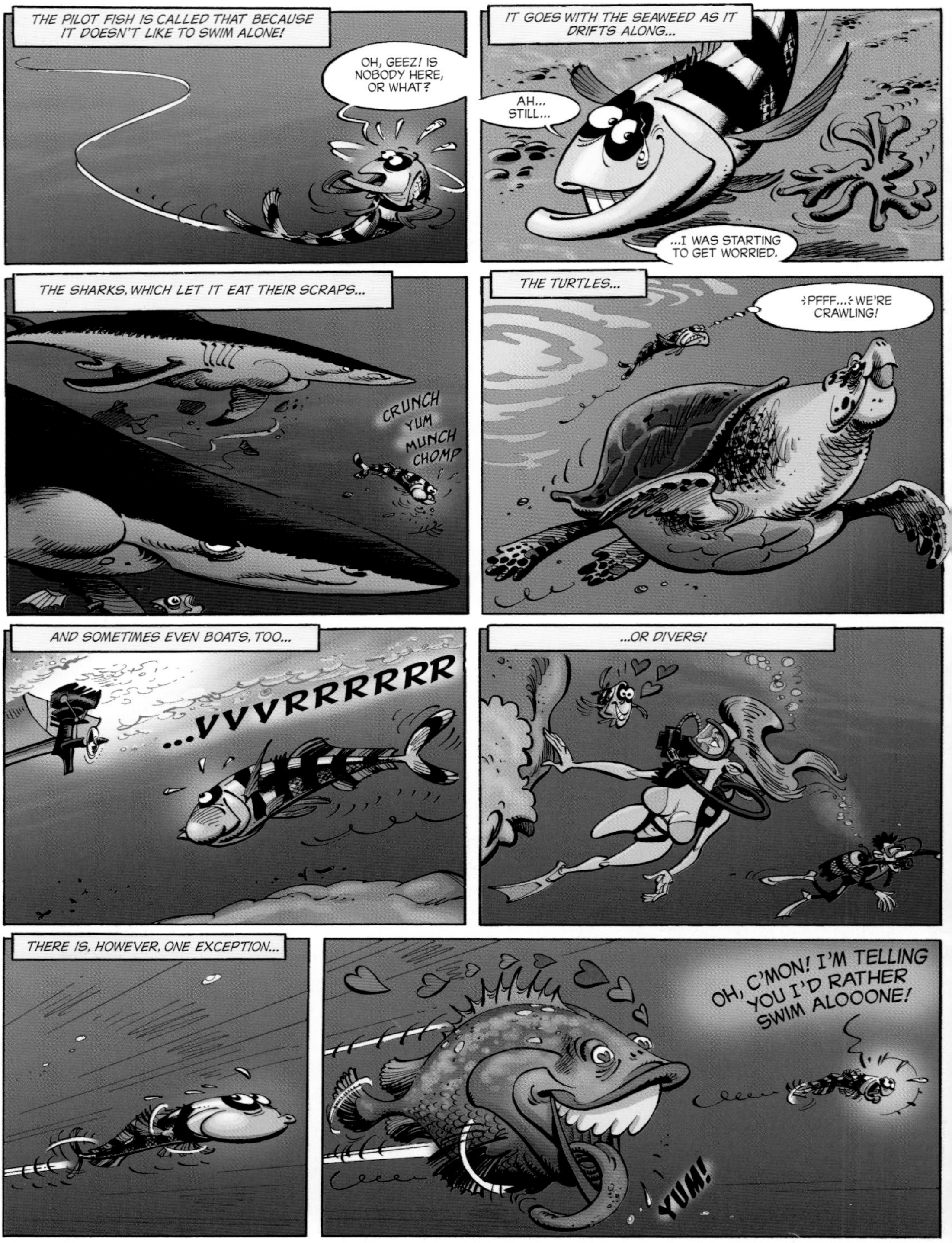

THE PILOT FISH IS CALLED THAT BECAUSE IT DOESN'T LIKE TO SWIM ALONE!
OH, GEEZ! IS NOBODY HERE, OR WHAT?
IT GOES WITH THE SEAWEED AS IT DRIFTS ALONG...
AH... STILL...
...I WAS STARTING TO GET WORRIED.
THE SHARKS, WHICH LET IT EAT THEIR SCRAPS...
CRUNCH
YUM
MUNCH
CHOMP
THE TURTLES...
PFFF... WE'RE CRAWLING!
AND SOMETIMES EVEN BOATS, TOO...
...VVVRRRRRRR
...OR DIVERS!
THERE IS, HOWEVER, ONE EXCEPTION...
OH, C'MON! I'M TELLING YOU I'D RATHER SWIM ALOOONE!
YUM!

THE PLASTIC CONTINENT

WHAT DO YOU THINK THIS NEW ISLAND IN THE MIDDLE OF THE PACIFIC OCEAN IS?

NOTHING MORE THAN A GIGANTIC OPEN-AIR TRASH CAN SIX TIMES THE SIZE OF FRANCE. WE CALL IT THE PLASTIC CONTINENT!

BROUGHT THERE BY THE CURRENTS, PLASTIC TRASH ACCUMULATES HERE AND ELSEWHERE IN THE OCEANS...

AND THAT'S HOW IT STARTS!

THIS HEAP ALSO PILES UP IN COLUMNS, SOMETIMES DOZENS OF FEET DEEP...

THE CONSEQUENCES FOR MARINE ANIMALS ARE **AWFUL!**

THEY SWALLOW TRASH...

...OR THEY GET ENTANGLED IN THE PLASTIC...

HELP... HELP...

THEY SUFFOCATE...

COUGH! COUGH! COUGH!

NOT TO MENTION THE MUTATIONS AFFECTING THE SPECIES THAT EAT IT!

EEEERRRREEEOOOO

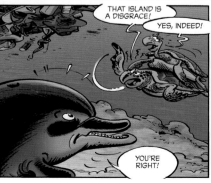

THAT ISLAND IS A DISGRACE!

YES, INDEED!

YOU'RE RIGHT!

IT'S HIDEOUS! IT STINKS! THAT'S THE LAST TIME WE'LL SPEND OUR VACATION HERE!

THE BROCHURE WAS A RIPOFF!

A JELLYFISH UNLIKE OTHERS

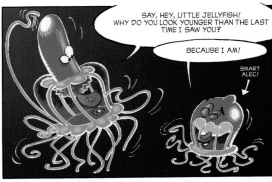

SAY, HEY, LITTLE JELLYFISH! WHY DO YOU LOOK YOUNGER THAN THE LAST TIME I SAW YOU?

BECAUSE I AM!

SMART ALEC!

IS THAT POSSIBLE?

YEAH--IT'S CALLED *TRANSDIFFERENTIATION!*

HEH-HEH!

WHEN I REACH ADULT AGE, MY BODY EXCHANGES ITS OLD CELLS FOR BRAND NEW CELLS. AS A RESULT, I REJUVENATE!

WOW...YOU'RE LUCKY!

"IT'S A LITTLE LIKE THE CUT-OFF TAIL OF A LIZARD THAT GROWS BACK, BUT FOR ME IT'S EVEN BETTER!"

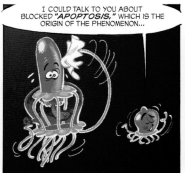

CRACK

HEY!

PRETTY CLASSY, ISN'T IT? HMM...?!

SNAR

ZAP

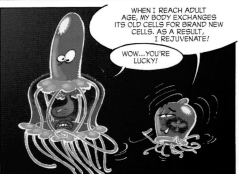

I'M THE ONLY *SPECIES IN THE WORLD* THAT'S TOTALLY "IMMORTAL"! TEMPTING, EH?

I COULD TALK TO YOU ABOUT BLOCKED *"APOPTOSIS,"* WHICH IS THE ORIGIN OF THE PHENOMENON...

OR EVEN ABOUT...ABOUT...

THE...

AND THEN...

THE...

?

I...

GOO?

THAT'S IT NOW! YOUR CELLS ARE STILL REJUVENATING, RIGHT?

YEAHHH, TOO CUTE! GO ON, GO BACK TO YOUR MOMMY QUICKLY--IT'S TIME FOR YOUR BOTTLE!

GA...GA... FL BL BLL BLL STUSS STUSS STUSS...

JELLYFISH
Turritopsis nutricula

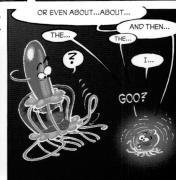

- **SIZE:** 5 millimeters [.2 inches]
- **DIET:** Zooplankton
- **DISTINCTIVE FEATURE:** This potentially immortal jellyfish is threatening to invade every sea in the world, no less!

DEPTH: 0-15 METERS [0-50 FEET]	NE*	GEOGRAPHICAL LOCATION

*THREATENED SPECIES RATING. SEE THE TABLE ON PAGE TWO.

WHO IS THE MOST DANGEROUS?

WHICH MARINE ANIMALS ARE THE MOST DANGEROUS TO HUMANS?

THERE ARE LOTS OF THEM! STARTING WITH THE MOST DREADED OF THEM ALL...

?

THE GREAT WHITE SHARK!

BBBLLDDBLL

BUT THERE'S ALSO THE STONE FISH AND ITS POISONOUS SPINES!

YEE-OOWWW!

THE BLUE-RINGED OCTOPUS, **TERRIBLY TOXIC!**

GAH

THE BARRACUDA, TIGER OF THE SEAS...

MUNCH

THE MORAY EEL AND ITS FORMIDABLE **BITE!**

GRAACK

THE WEEVER THAT **STINGS** THE FEET OF SWIMMERS...

OOWWWWWIIIIEEEE

THE JELLYFISH—TOUCHING IT IS ENOUGH TO SUFFER FROM TERRIBLE ITCHING...

THE STINGRAY, WHOSE BITE CAN LEAD TO INFECTIONS...

THE CATFISH, WHICH IS ALSO VERY POISONOUS...

THE ELECTRIC EEL...

THE SURGEON FISH—THE BASE OF ITS TAIL CUTS LIKE A SCALPEL, ETC., ETC.

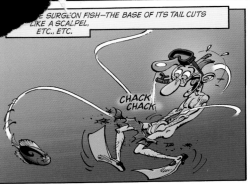

CONVERSELY, IT'S QUICKER TO NAME THE WORST PREDATORS FOR MARINE ANIMALS...

THERE'S ONLY ONE: HUMANS!

BIOMIMETICS

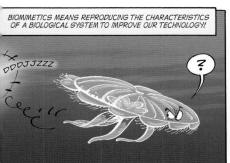

BIOMIMETICS MEANS REPRODUCING THE CHARACTERISTICS OF A BIOLOGICAL SYSTEM TO IMPROVE OUR TECHNOLOGY!

DDDJJZZZ

?

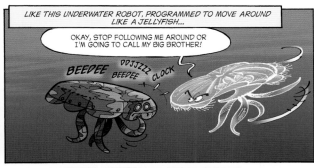

LIKE THIS UNDERWATER ROBOT, PROGRAMMED TO MOVE AROUND LIKE A JELLYFISH...

OKAY, STOP FOLLOWING ME AROUND OR I'M GOING TO CALL MY BIG BROTHER!

BEEDEE DDJJZZZ BEEDEE CLOCK

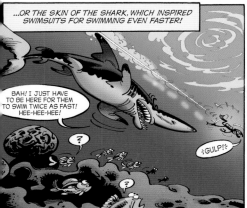

...OR THE SKIN OF THE SHARK, WHICH INSPIRED SWIMSUITS FOR SWIMMING EVEN FASTER!

BAH! I JUST HAVE TO BE HERE FOR THEM TO SWIM TWICE AS FAST! HEE-HEE-HEE!

?

?

GULP!

THIS MILITARY ARMOR COPIES THE ABILITIES OF PEARLY MOLLUSKS!

AS FOR THE FORM, ON THE OTHER HAND...

?

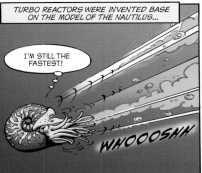

TURBO REACTORS WERE INVENTED BASE ON THE MODEL OF THE NAUTILUS...

I'M STILL THE FASTEST!

WHOOOSHH

GLUE MANUFACTURERS ARE INTERESTED IN STICKY THREADS MADE BY MUSSELS, ETC.

IT'S NOT YET QUITE FINALIZED...

IN FACT, HUMANITY SPENDS ITS TIME IMITATING ANIMALS...

AAAAR

HA! HA! HA!

...AND MAYBE THE REVERSE IS ALSO THE CASE!

MY TURN! MY TURN TO MAKE YOU GUESS!

EASY! THAT'S A HUMAN WHO STEPPED ON A BEAR CUB!

HA! HA! HA! HA!

HOO! HOO! HOO!

HEE! HEE! HEE!

WRECKFISH

...AND RIGHT BELOW US, OCEANA, IS THE WRECKAGE OF A 15TH CENTURY GALLEON!

I REALLY WOULD HAVE LIKED TO VISIT IT WITH MY FATHER...

ME, TOO! THOSE SHIPS WERE FILLED WITH TREASURE...

"WITH COFFERS STUFFED WITH GOLD COINS...

"WITH EXTRAORDINARY JEWELS, PRECIOUS GEMSTONES...

"AMPHORAE FULL OF DIAMONDS...

"BULLION, WORKS OF ART..."

SOMETHING LIKE TENS AND TENS OF MILLIONS OF THEM...!

WOW!

HEY, LOOK AT THE TREASURE I FOUND!

$$

WHAT WE CALL A WRECKFISH! I'VE WANTED TO STUDY ONE UP CLOSE FOR THE LONGEST TIME!

I'M SO HAPPY!

FLAP FLAP FLAP

LUCKY

THE GIANT SQUID, A LIVING LEGEND

FOR A LONG TIME, THE GIANT SQUID REMAINED A CREATURE OF LEGEND...

THE TERRIFYING KRAKEN

VERY FEW HUMANS HAD SEEN IT ALIVE...

FORGET IT. IT'S A MYTH!

I SWEAR TO YOU. IT WAS *ENORMOUS!*

WHATEVER!

HOW DOES IT MOVE AROUND? WE WEREN'T REALLY SURE ABOUT THAT...

?

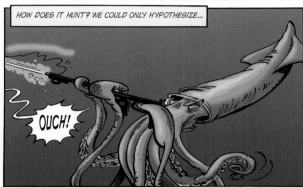
HOW DOES IT HUNT? WE COULD ONLY HYPOTHESIZE...

OUCH!

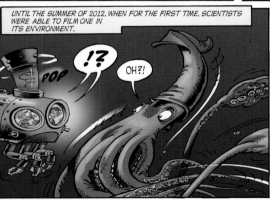
UNTIL THE SUMMER OF 2012, WHEN FOR THE FIRST TIME, SCIENTISTS WERE ABLE TO FILM ONE IN ITS ENVIRONMENT.

POP

!?

OH?!

OH, MY GOODNESS! OH, MY GRACIOUS! YOU'LL NEVER GUESS, GUYS!

WHAT?

J-JUST SAW SOME HUMANS!

WHATEVER!

NO ONE'S EVER SEEN THEM ALIVE!

FORGET IT. THEY'RE A MYTH!

GIANT SQUID
Architeuthis dux

- **SIZE:** 12-20 meters [40-65 FEET]
- **DIET:** Carnivore
- **DISTINCTIVE FEATURE:** Via the lightning produced at the ends of its arms, it blinds its prey to catch it more easily.

DEPTH: 200-1000 METERS [650-3300 FEET]	NE*	GEOGRAPHICAL LOCATION

*THREATENED SPECIES RATING. SEE THE TABLE ON PAGE TWO.

AN EXCEPTIONALLY GIFTED OCTOPUS

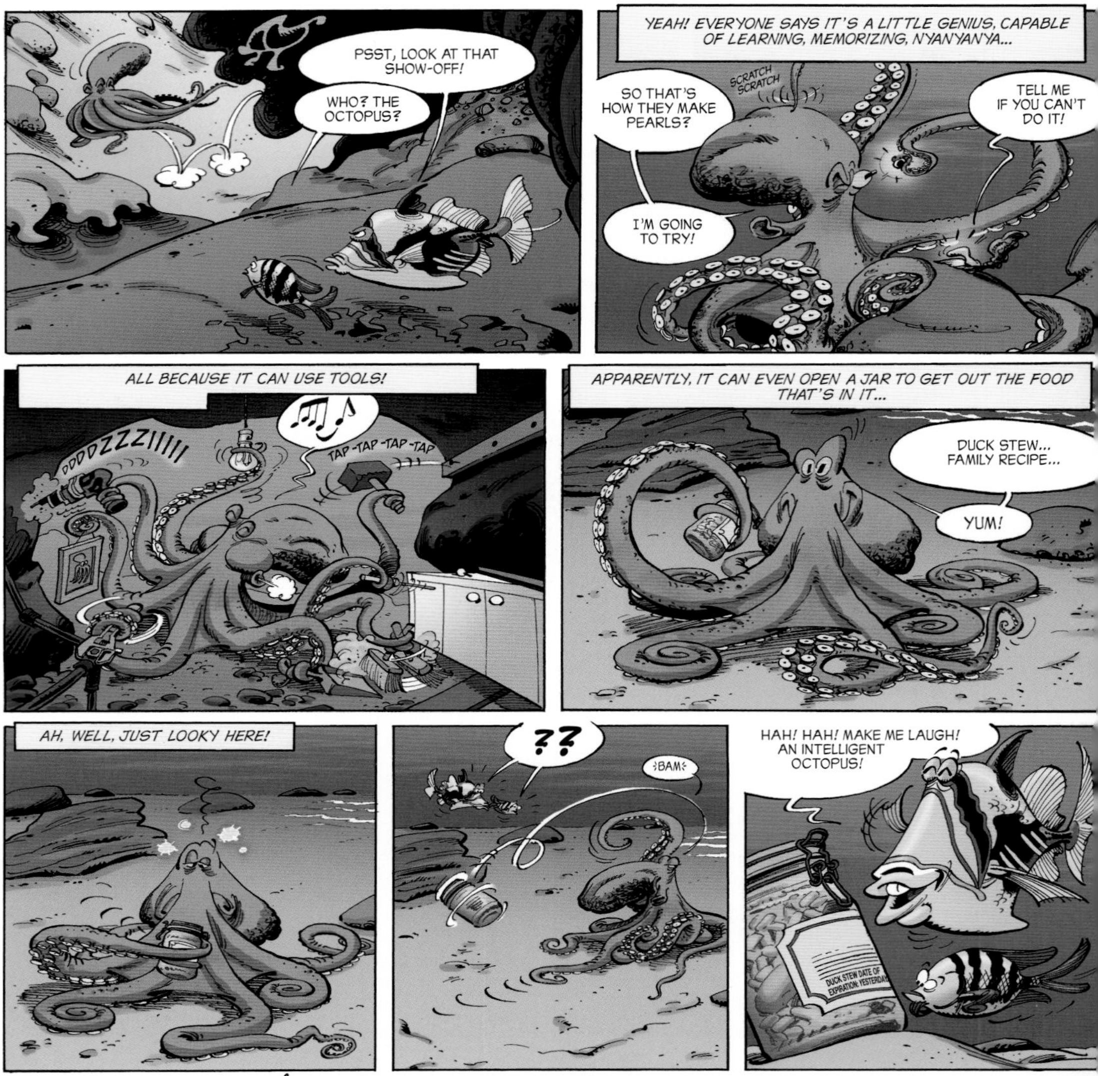

PSST, LOOK AT THAT SHOW-OFF!
WHO? THE OCTOPUS?
YEAH! EVERYONE SAYS IT'S A LITTLE GENIUS, CAPABLE OF LEARNING, MEMORIZING, N'YAN'YAN'YA...
SCRATCH SCRATCH
SO THAT'S HOW THEY MAKE PEARLS?
TELL ME IF YOU CAN'T DO IT!
I'M GOING TO TRY!
ALL BECAUSE IT CAN USE TOOLS!
DDDDZZZZIIIII
TAP-TAP-TAP-TAP
APPARENTLY, IT CAN EVEN OPEN A JAR TO GET OUT THE FOOD THAT'S IN IT...
DUCK STEW... FAMILY RECIPE...
YUM!
AH, WELL, JUST LOOKY HERE!
??
BAM
HAH! HAH! MAKE ME LAUGH! AN INTELLIGENT OCTOPUS!
DUCK STEW DATE OF EXPIRATION: YESTERDAY

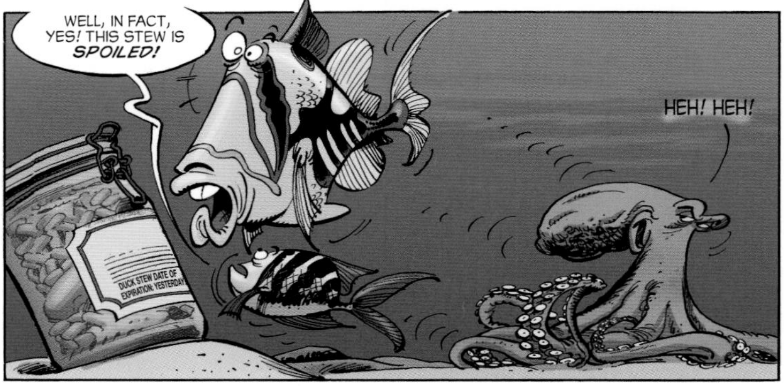

WELL, IN FACT, YES! THIS STEW IS SPOILED!
HEH! HEH!
DUCK STEW DATE OF EXPIRATION: YESTERDAY

COMMON OCTOPUS

Octopus vulgaris

- **SIZE:** Up to 1 meter [3 feet] (including tentacles)
- **DIET:** Carnivore (Crustaceans)
- **DISTINCTIVE FEATURE:** Endowed with a rare intelligence, the octopus would undoubtedly dominate the seas if it didn't die shortly after mating.

DEPTH: 0-150 METERS [0-500 FEET] | NE* | GEOGRAPHICAL LOCATION

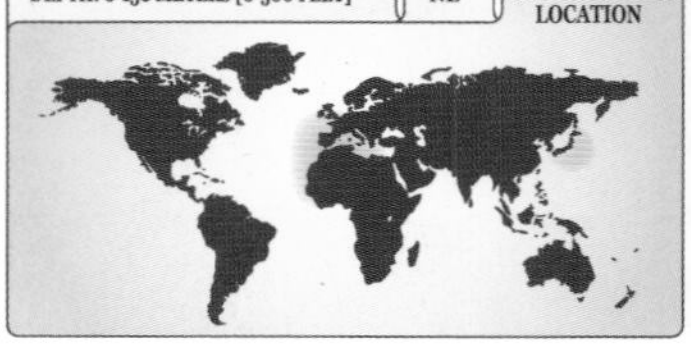

*THREATENED SPECIES RATING. SEE THE TABLE ON PAGE TWO.

VICTIMS OF THEIR SUCCESS

WHEN THE CLOWN FISH BECAME A MOVIE STAR, EVERYONE WANTED ONE IN THEIR AQUARIUMS...

WERE YOU IN THE MOVIE, TOO?

?

JAWS INSPIRED SHARK PHOBIA...

WANTED!

DEAD OR NOT ALIVE!

IS THAT YOU IN THE PHOTO, DADDY?

THE SUCCESS OF THE FLIPPER TV SERIES INCREASED THE NUMBERS OF DOLPHINS CAPTURED TO FILL AQUATIC PARKS...

IF I EVER GET HOLD OF THAT ⊙✱✤☢⊛☠!! FLIPPER...!

WHALES NEVER FELT CALM AGAIN AFTER MOBY DICK...

DID YOU READ THAT BOOK?

NO, THERE'S NOT A WATERPROOF VERSION!

LOTS OF OTHERS HAVE BEEN THE VICTIMS OF THEIR OWN SUCCESS, LIKE TURTLES AFTER THE MOVIE SAMMY...

WHO WANTS THEIR TURTLE EGG?!

BUT I JUST LAID THEM ALL!

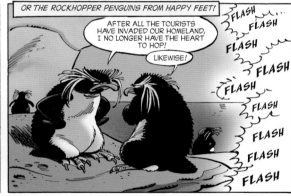

OR THE ROCKHOPPER PENGUINS FROM HAPPY FEET!

AFTER ALL THE TOURISTS HAVE INVADED OUR HOMELAND, I NO LONGER HAVE THE HEART TO HOP!

LIKEWISE!

FLASH FLASH FLASH FLASH FLASH FLASH FLASH FLASH FLASH

ALL THE SAME, IT'S GETTING HARDER TO FIND NEW CANDIDATES!

NO WONDER...

BECOME A BIG STAR IN THE WORLD OF HUMANS— GRAND CASTING!

NOT ON YOUR LIFE!

THE WORST PIRANHA

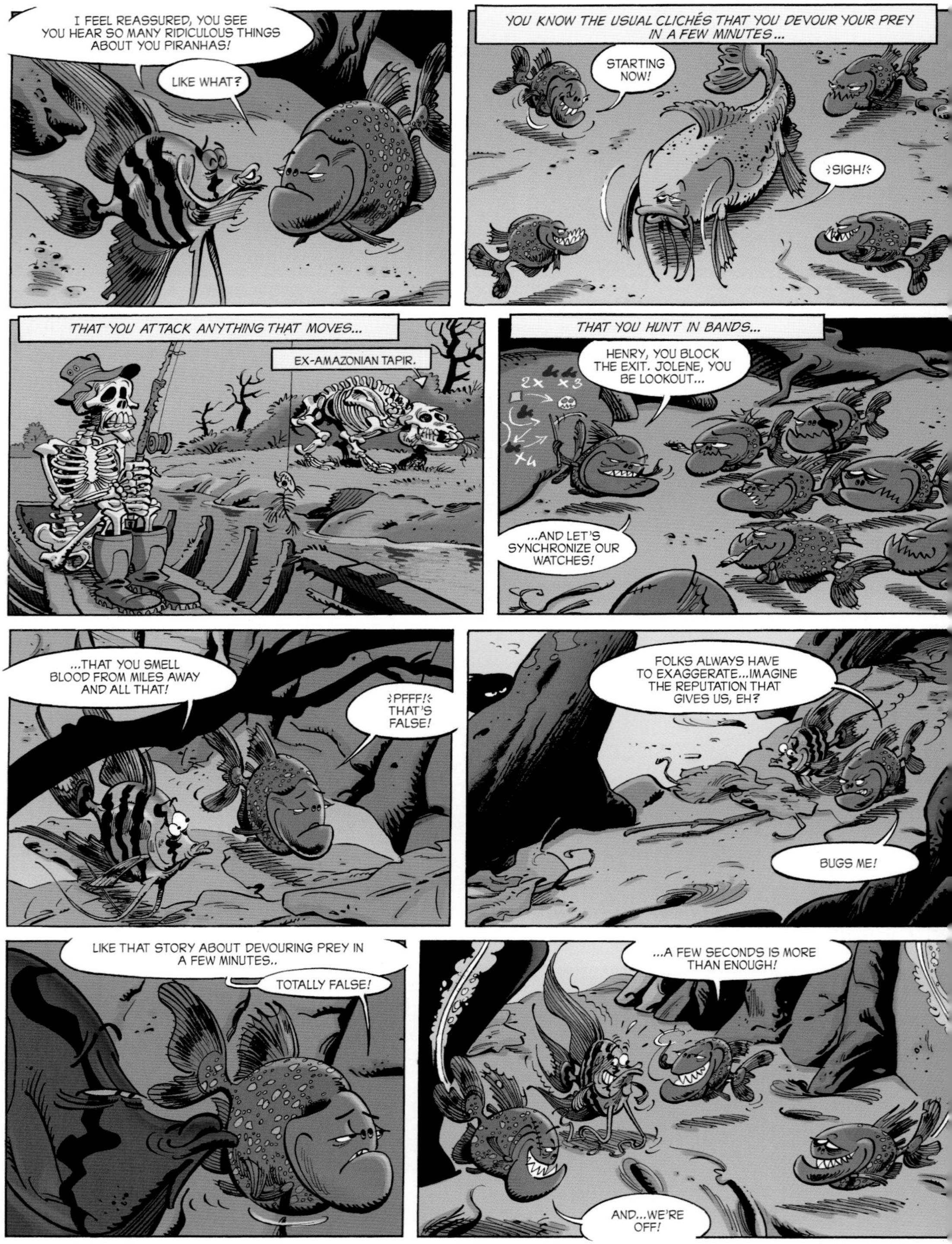
I FEEL REASSURED, YOU SEE YOU HEAR SO MANY RIDICULOUS THINGS ABOUT YOU PIRANHAS!
LIKE WHAT?
YOU KNOW THE USUAL CLICHÉS THAT YOU DEVOUR YOUR PREY IN A FEW MINUTES...
STARTING NOW!
SIGH!
THAT YOU ATTACK ANYTHING THAT MOVES...
EX-AMAZONIAN TAPIR.
THAT YOU HUNT IN BANDS...
HENRY, YOU BLOCK THE EXIT. JOLENE, YOU BE LOOKOUT...
...AND LET'S SYNCHRONIZE OUR WATCHES!
...THAT YOU SMELL BLOOD FROM MILES AWAY AND ALL THAT!
PFFF! THAT'S FALSE!
FOLKS ALWAYS HAVE TO EXAGGERATE...IMAGINE THE REPUTATION THAT GIVES US, EH?
BUGS ME!
LIKE THAT STORY ABOUT DEVOURING PREY IN A FEW MINUTES..
TOTALLY FALSE!
...A FEW SECONDS IS MORE THAN ENOUGH!
AND...WE'RE OFF!

THE HERMIT CRAB

IF THERE'S ONE SPECIES THAT ANNOYS ME, IT'S DEFINITELY THE HERMIT CRAB!

YOU KNOW, THE CRUSTACEAN THAT HAS A SOFT ABDOMEN AND DOESN'T HAVE A SHELL!

WAH...I NEED TO FIND A SPOT TO HAVE SIESTA!

TO BEDDY-BYE!

AS A RESULT, IT SPENDS ALL ITS TIME SQUATTING IN OTHERS' HOMES! IT COULD BELONG TO A SPONGE...

THIS ONE SCRATCHES A BIT!

A GASTROPOD'S SHELL...

WOW, IT EVEN HAS A JACUZZI!

OR THE FIRST SPACE IT FINDS...

THESE MODERN APARTMENTS AREN'T SO TERRIBLE...

IT THINKS EVERYTHING'S ALLOWED!

BAH, LIVE AND LET LIVE! AS LONG AS IT DOESN'T ANNOY US...

EXACTLY!

HA!

HEY-HO, THE DOOR! IT'S FREEZING IN HERE!

HERMIT CRAB
Pagurus bernardus

- **SIZE:** 5-10 centimeters [2-4 inches]
- **DIET:** Omnivore, Detritivore
- **DISTINCTIVE FEATURE:** It finds empty shells to occupy in order to protect its very soft abdomen.

DEPTH: 0-500 METERS [0-1600 FEET]	DD*	GEOGRAPHICAL LOCATION

*THREATENED SPECIES RATING. SEE THE TABLE ON PAGE TWO.

A WHOLE WORLD UNDER THE SAND

THE BEACH IS WORTHLESS AT LOW TIDE... NOTHING TO SEE!

DO YOU THINK SO? GO ON AND DIG UNDER THE SAND A LITTLE, THEN!

OH? THERE'RE SOME THINGS MOVING AROUND!

OF COURSE! IT'S FULL OF LIVING CREATURES!

EVEN DOWN THERE!

HERE'S THE SEA URCHIN. IT LIKES TO LIVE BURIED AWAY, HIDDEN FROM VIEW!

?

AND HERE'S A **SAND MASON** WORM! BY GATHERING GRAINS OF SAND AROUND ITS BODY, IT MAKES ITSELF A PROTECTIVE TUBE.

MORE THAN A TUBE--IT'S A **WORK OF ART!**

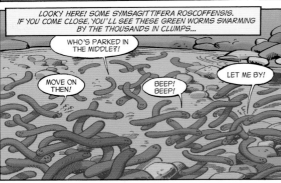

LOOKY HERE! SOME SYMSAGITTIFERA ROSCOFFENSIS. IF YOU COME CLOSE, YOU'LL SEE THESE GREEN WORMS SWARMING BY THE THOUSANDS IN CLUMPS...

WHO'S PARKED IN THE MIDDLE?!

MOVE ON THEN!

BEEP! BEEP!

LET ME BY!

NOT TO MENTION THE SHELLFISH, RAZOR CLAMS, LITTLE CRABS, AND ALL THEIR MICROSCOPIC COLLEAGUES...

FOLLOW ME! WE'LL NOW GO EXAMNINE ROCKS UP CLOSE AND PERSONAL!

WAIT!

IT WOULD BE MORE COMFORTABLE FOR THEM TO LIVE INSIDE HERE, DON'T YOU THINK?

SALMON'S SIXTH SENSE

WE SALMON ARE ABLE TO FIND THE EXACT PLACE WHERE WE CAME OUT OF THE EGG!

SERIOUSLY?

FOLLOW ME AND YOU'LL SEE! I FIND MY WAY USING THE EARTH'S MAGNETIC FIELD!

I'LL EXPLAIN IT TO YOU...

I ALSO USE CELESTIAL NAVIGATION...

HMM... MARS IS ALIGNED WITH VENUS... OKAY...

I ALSO USE THE SUNLIGHT...

PHEW

IT'S AN IMMEDIATE LEFT AFTER THE SUN...

...AND I PICK OUT THE SCENTS FROM WHEN I WAS LITTLE FROM THE WATER MOLECULES!

SNIFF SNIFF SNIFF

AH...THAT SMELLS LIKE DIAPERS!

HA! HA!

AND THERE YOU GO! THIS IS EXACTLY WHERE I CAME OUT OF THE EGG!

SNIFF

SO, ARE YOU AMAZED?

OBVIOUSLY!

PARTICULARLY, I'M, WONDERING WHERE YOU FOUND SUCH A LONG THREAD?

TEE-HEE!

ATLANTIC SALMON
Salmo salar

- **SIZE:** 50-140 centimeters [20-55 inches]
- **DIET:** Carnivore
- **DISTINCTIVE FEATURE:** Often enough the birth of a salmon coincides with the death of its parents. Not a happy story...

DEPTH: 0-40 METERS [0-130 FEET]	NT*	GEOGRAPHICAL LOCATION

*THREATENED SPECIES RATING. SEE THE TABLE ON PAGE TWO.

A MULTICOLORED CUTTLEFISH

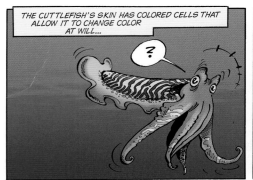

THE CUTTLEFISH'S SKIN HAS COLORED CELLS THAT ALLOW IT TO CHANGE COLOR AT WILL...

?

VERY USEFUL FOR ESCAPING A PREDATOR...

...OR FOR NOT BEING SEEN BY PREY!

SOMETIMES IT CHOOSES LIVELIER COLORS...

SCRAT SCRAT

...WHICH MAY BE THE BASIS OF A VISUAL LANGUAGE THAT SCIENTISTS ARE JUST NOW BEGINNING TO INTERPRET.

WAFWAFWAF

HEE! HEE! HEE!

EXCELLENT! EXCELLENT!

NOT VERY APPEALING TO THE GIRLS, BUT GOOD...

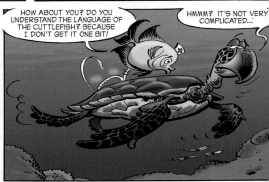

HOW ABOUT YOU? DO YOU UNDERSTAND THE LANGUAGE OF THE CUTTLEFISH? BECAUSE I DON'T GET IT ONE BIT!

HMMM? IT'S NOT VERY COMPLICATED...

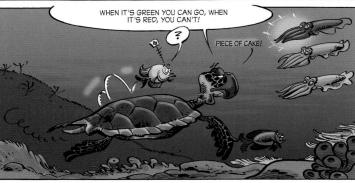

WHEN IT'S GREEN YOU CAN GO, WHEN IT'S RED, YOU CAN'T!

?

PIECE OF CAKE!

COMMON CUTTLEFISH
Sepia officinalus

- **SIZE:** 40 centimeters [16 inches]
- **DIET:** Carnivore
- **DISTINCTIVE FEATURE:** To keep from being confu the cuttlefish has a bone, the squid has a pen, and the octopus has no skeleton at all.

DEPTH: 0-150 METERS [0-500 FEET]	NE*	GEOGRAPHICAL LOCATION

*THREATENED SPECIES RATING. SEE THE TABLE ON PAGE TWO.

THE PEOPLE OF THE ABYSS

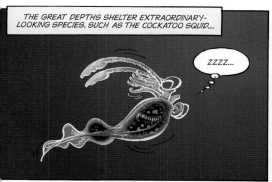

THE GREAT DEPTHS SHELTER EXTRAORDINARY-LOOKING SPECIES, SUCH AS THE COCKATOO SQUID...

ZZZZ...

THE PACIFIC VIPERFISH, WHOSE TEETH KEEP ITS PREY FROM FLEEING...

THEY KEEP ME FROM SEEING CLEARLY, TOO!

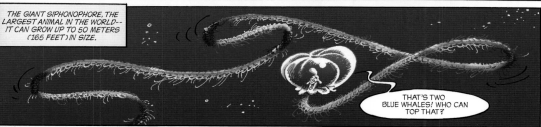

THE GIANT SIPHONOPHORE, THE LARGEST ANIMAL IN THE WORLD-- IT CAN GROW UP TO 50 METERS (165 FEET) IN SIZE.

THAT'S TWO BLUE WHALES! WHO CAN TOP THAT?

THE VAMPIRE OF THE ABYSS--THE WHITE, ABYSSAL VAMPIRE SQUID...

BOO!

AAAHHH...

THE DUMBO OCTOPUS, THE SLENDER BLACKSMELT...

THE LANTERN FISH, THE SNAILFISH...

AND THIS SORT OF SARDINE WITH SPIKY BARBS...

?

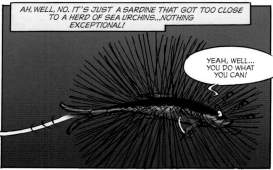

AH, WELL, NO. IT'S JUST A SARDINE THAT GOT TOO CLOSE TO A HERD OF SEA URCHINS...NOTHING EXCEPTIONAL!

YEAH, WELL... YOU DO WHAT YOU CAN!

PRESERVING THE OCEANS

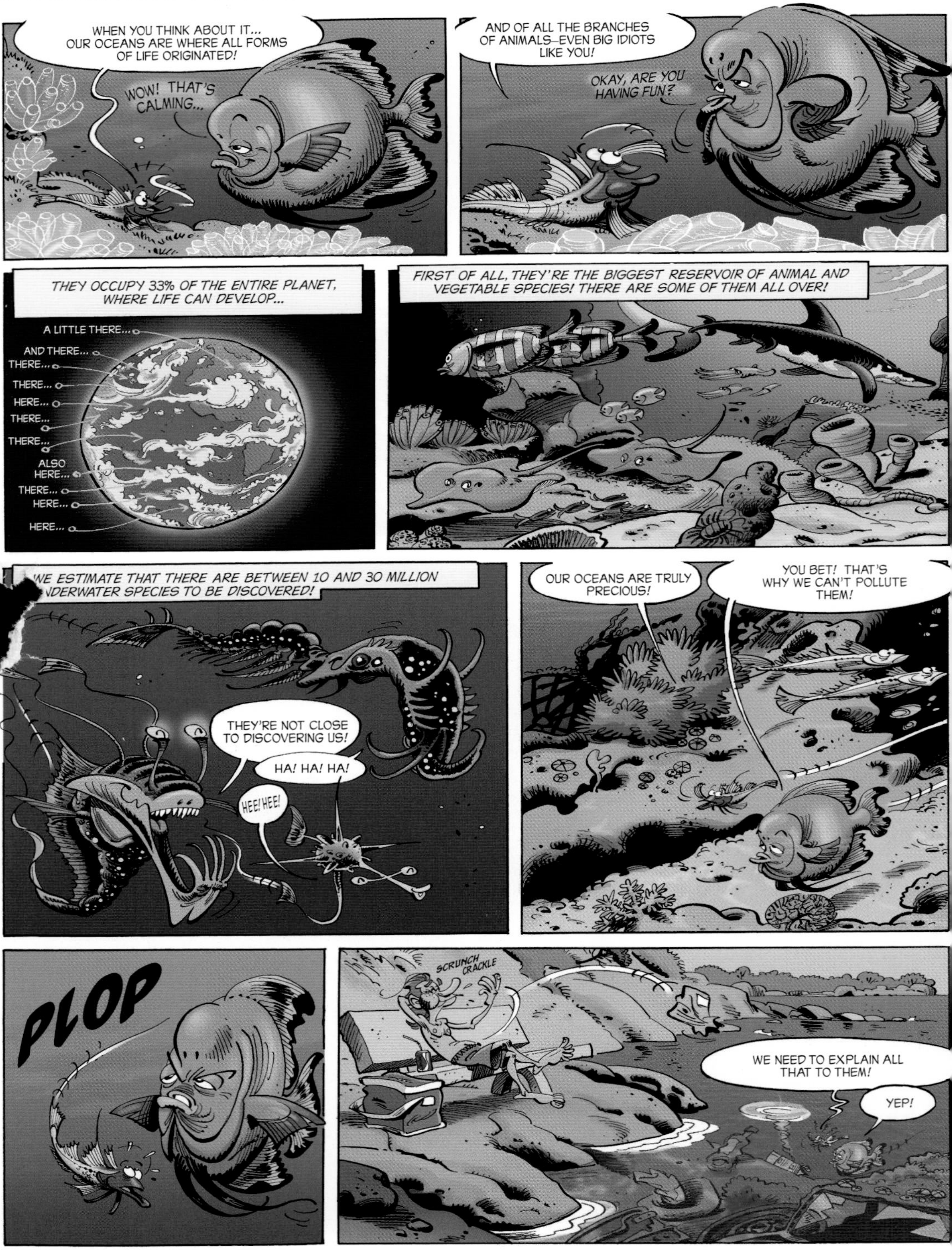

WHEN YOU THINK ABOUT IT... OUR OCEANS ARE WHERE ALL FORMS OF LIFE ORIGINATED!
WOW! THAT'S CALMING...
AND OF ALL THE BRANCHES OF ANIMALS—EVEN BIG IDIOTS LIKE YOU!
OKAY, ARE YOU HAVING FUN?
THEY OCCUPY 33% OF THE ENTIRE PLANET, WHERE LIFE CAN DEVELOP...
A LITTLE THERE...
AND THERE...
THERE...
THERE...
HERE...
THERE...
THERE...
ALSO HERE...
THERE...
HERE...
HERE...
FIRST OF ALL, THEY'RE THE BIGGEST RESERVOIR OF ANIMAL AND VEGETABLE SPECIES! THERE ARE SOME OF THEM ALL OVER!
WE ESTIMATE THAT THERE ARE BETWEEN 10 AND 30 MILLION NDERWATER SPECIES TO BE DISCOVERED!
THEY'RE NOT CLOSE TO DISCOVERING US!
HA! HA! HA!
HEE! HEE!
OUR OCEANS ARE TRULY PRECIOUS!
YOU BET! THAT'S WHY WE CAN'T POLLUTE THEM!
PLOP
SCRUNCH
CRACKLE
WE NEED TO EXPLAIN ALL THAT TO THEM!
YEP!

WATCH OUT FOR PAPERCUTZ™

Welcome aboard the fish-filled, first SEA CREATURES IN THEIR OWN WORDS graphic novel by Christophe Cazenove and Thierry Jytéry from Papercutz, those loose-lipped, landlubbers dedicated to publishing great graphic novels for all ages. I'm Jim Salicrup, Editor-in-Chief and your comicbook Captain on this maiden voyage to the bottom of the sea.

This graphic novel is all about getting to know the marine animals that live in the oceans all over the world—those mysterious creatures with whom we share the planet. Being in comics format, the creators have taken artistic license and have allowed those creatures to directly tell you their stories in their owns words. So instead of being a dull, stodgy illustrated text book, all the fascinating facts about our undersea friends are delivered to you in a fun, original way. Not unlike DINOSAURS, another great Papercutz graphic novel series (by Plumeri and Bloz). In DINOSAURS, we were guided back in time by Indino Jones to the days when dinosaurs walked the Earth. Each DINOSAURS graphic novel was cram-packed with

up-to-date facts about every type of dinosaur that ever existed, yet told in the imaginary voices of the great creatures themselves. To give you a better idea of exactly what we're talking about, we're presenting as an extra-special bonus—pages from DINOSAURS #1 "In the Beginning..." starting on the very next page. We're hoping that if you enjoy SEA CREATURES you'll also appreciate the comics in DINOSAURS.

But it doesn't end there! At Papercutz once we get on a particular subject—especially one that captures the imagination the way dinosaurs do—we tend to want to explore it further in every way possible. While the DINOSAURS graphic novels are about imparting factual information, we decided to start an all-new graphic novel series about the possibility of dinosaurs living among us today! It's a very different approach than the one seen in the exciting Jurassic Park movies (long-time comics fans might remember I edited the original Jurassic Park comics way back when!), it involves dinosaurs that are somewhat humanoid—and really can speak! It's a new series we're working on at Papercutz called MANOSAURS and we're betting you're going to love it! I can't show you anything on it just yet, but keep an eye on Papercutz.com for an exciting announcement and further information.

Back to SEA CREATURES, believe it or not, I'm hopeful that this graphic novel will inspire you in some way. When Ringo Starr first learned that "octopuses travel along the sea bed picking up stones and shiny objects with which to build gardens," he was inspired to write and sing the Beatles hit, "Octopus's Garden," a favorite song of mine. Who knows what this graphic novel (or SEA CREATURES #2 "Armed and Dangerous," coming soon to a bookseller or library near you!) may inspire you to create?!

Thanks, Jim

STAY IN TOUCH!

EMAIL: salicrup@papercutz.com
WEB: www.papercutz.com
TWITTER: @papercutzgn
FACEBOOK: PAPERCUTZGRAPHICNOVELS
REGULAR MAIL: Papercutz, 160 Broadway, Suite 700, East Wing, New York, NY 10038

RECORDS

YOU WANT TO LEARN ABOUT DINOSAUR RECORDS? ASK INDINO JONES!

THAT'S ME, HEE, HEE!

FASTEST DINOSAUR? GALLIMIMUS, WITH SPRINTS OF UP TO 40 MPH!

PTOUEY! PTOUEY!

UGH! THE PROBLEM IS THAT I SWALLOW LOTS OF MOSQUITOES!

YUCK!

LONGEST DINOSAUR? ARGENTINOSAURUS, NO DOUBT-- 130 FEET LONG!

AND AS FOR CARNIVORES, GIGANOTOSAURUS WAS ONE OF THE MOST MASSIVE (46 FEET, 17,636 LBS).

YUM! THERE'S AT LEAST A YEAR OF GRUB OVER THERE!

SMALLEST DINOSAUR? MICRORAPTOR-- 16 INCHES LONG!

HEY!

THAT'S NO REASON TO STICK ME IN A TINY LITTLE PANEL!

SMARTEST DINOSAUR? TROODON WAS AS SMART AS A CAT!

HEE! HEE!

THAT'S WHY I BURY MY DROPPINGS!

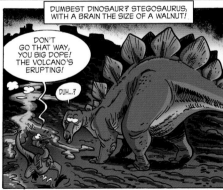

DUMBEST DINOSAUR? STEGOSAURUS, WITH A BRAIN THE SIZE OF A WALNUT!

DON'T GO THAT WAY, YOU BIG DOPE! THE VOLCANO'S ERUPTING!

DUH...?

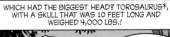

WHICH HAD THE BIGGEST HEAD? TOROSAURUS*, WITH A SKULL THAT WAS 10 FEET LONG AND WEIGHED 4,000 LBS.!

TALK ABOUT A STIFF NECK...

OH, YEAH! BECAUSE, IN MY OPINION, SOMEONE WHO REALLY HAS A BIG HEAD...

IS A GUY WHO REFUSES TO TAKE OUT THE TRASH OR WALK THE DOG!

IF IT'S A QUESTION OF LAZINESS, YOU BREAK ALL THE RECORDS!

CALM DOWN, DEAREST, I'M GOING!

PLUMERI & BLOZ

*EXPERTS HAVE FOUND THAT TOROSAURUS MIGHT HAVE ACTUALLY BEEN AN ADULT TRICERATOPS.

Dinosaures [Dinosaurs] by Arnaud Plumeri & Bloz © 2010 BAMBOO ÉDITION. www.bamboo.fr

THE FIRST DINOSAURS

WELCOME TO THE *TRIASSIC*, 230 MILLION YEARS AGO...

HEY, GUYS! COME SEE WHAT I FOUND!

?

?

SOME OLD REPTILES BUMP INTO SOMETHING THAT WILL CHANGE THEIR LIVES...

I MUST BE SEEING THINGS.

WHAT'S THIS IRRITATING THINGAMAJIG?

HUH?

...ONE OF THE FIRST DINOSAURS: *EORAPTOR.*

HOW ABOUT A LITTLE RESPECT, GUYS!

I DON'T SEE ANYTHING SPECIAL ABOUT THIS DINO-THINGY...

IS THAT A JOKE, BUDDY?!

FIRST OF ALL, I WALK ON TWO LEGS...

...WHICH NOT EVERYONE GETS TO DO...

BZZZZ

AND WHICH LETS ME BE SUPER SWIFT WHEN HUNTING!

CLAP

GULP

PLUS I'VE GOT POTENTIAL!

IN A FEW YEARS, I'VE GOT A HUNCH I'M GOING TO BECOME EXTRA HUGE!

GROW RRR

T. Rex

NO WAY!

GO ON, GET OUTTA HERE!

JUST A FAD, THESE DINOSAURS!

OOFF

THAT'S NEVER GOING TO HAPPEN!

HOPE-LESS!

WHAT AN IDIOT!

YOU'RE NOT GOING TO BE SO BIG IN A FEW MILLION YEARS!

SADLY FOR THEM, THESE OLD REPTILES WILL SOON GIVE WAY TO THE AMBITIOUS DINOSAURS.

PLUMERI / BLOZ

TYRANNOSAURUS REX

LET'S TAKE A LOOK AT THIS SULLEN LITTLE DINOSAUR...

HEY, GUYS, CHECK OUT WHO'S TURNED UP! IT'S THE LITTLE RUNT!

HI, LITTLE RUNT! YOU'RE UGLY, YOU KNOW THAT?

...IT DOESN'T LOOK LIKE HE HAS AN EASY LIFE...

SO, UGLY DUCKLING, YOU'RE WALKING AROUND LIKE A GROWNUP?

YOU DO KNOW YOU COULD GET YOURSELF INTO SOME TROUBLE?

:GRUMMBLLLE:

GET OUT OF MY TERRITORY, YOU UGLY, LITTLE RUNT!

YUM! A JUICY LITTLE FLEDGLING!

WAAAH!

FLAP FLAP FLAP

SUCH TRAGIC SCENES, BUT SOON THE TABLES WILL TURN!

AT ADOLESCENCE, OUR LITTLE DINOSAUR WILL LOSE HIS FEATHERS...

?

AND WILL GROW AND GROW INTO A TERRIFYING TYRANNOSAURUS REX!

ROAR

A DIFFICULT CHILDHOOD... COULD THAT BE THE REASON FOR T. REX'S NASTY TEMPER? IT'S A MYSTERY!

ROOOOAR

WHY'S HE SO MEAN?

TYRANNOSAURUS REX

MEANING: TYRANT LIZARD KING
PERIOD: LATE CRETACEOUS (68-65 MILLION YEARS AGO)
ORDER/ FAMILY: SAURISCHIA / TYRANNOSAURIDAE
SIZE: 35-50 FEET LONG
WEIGHT: 11,000 POUNDS
DIET: CARNIVORE
FOUND: NORTH AMERICA

T. PLUMERI & BLOZ·REX

WHAT'S A DINOSAUR?

DINOSAUR IS A TERM INVENTED BY **SIR RICHARD OWEN.** IT MEANS "FEARFULLY GREAT LIZARD," IN GREEK.

"FEARFULLY GREAT LIZARD?" HA! HE MUST HAVE NEVER MET YOU, COMPSO!

WE'VE IDENTIFIED OVER 1000 DINOSAUR SPECIES, AND PALEONTOLOGISTS DISCOVER ABOUT A DOZEN MORE EVERY YEAR.

OBSERVE, "LITTLE GUY!" HERE'S MY LATEST DISCOVERY... ...A FRAGMENT OF THE SKULL OF A FEMALE FLEABAGASUS!

UH, BOSS... I THINK THAT'S JUST A DRIED COW PATTY...

THESE CREATURES RULED THE EARTH FOR A LONG PERIOD: FROM BETWEEN 230-65 MILLION YEARS AGO. THUS, TYRANNOSAURUS DID NOT LIVE IN THE SAME TIME PERIOD AS COMPSOGNATHUS...

≻PHEW!≺ THAT'S A RELIEF!

UNFORTUNATELY FOR THEM, COMPSOGNATHUS COULD ENCOUNTER ANOTHER MONSTER: ALLOSAURUS...

ALLOSAURUS?! THIS IS WORSE!

MOMMY!

UNLIKE TODAY'S REPTILES, DINOSAURS DID NOT CRAWL: THEY WALKED UPRIGHT ON 2 OR 4 LEGS.

ARE YOU GOING TO CRAWL BEFORE YOUR MASTER, LITTLE WORM?

ON MY MOTHER'S LIFE, I CAN'T, SIR! SCIENCE SAYS SO!

AS FOR DIET, SOME DINOSAURS WERE **HERBIVORES** (PLANT EATERS) AND OTHERS WERE **CARNIVORES** (MEAT EATERS).

I'M NOT PICKY! I LIKE *ALL* DINOSAURS!

BUT I'M TELLING YOU I TASTE AWFUL!

HELP!

WITH SPINES, HORNS, AND ARMOR, DINOSAURS COULD HAVE GREATLY DIFFERING AND SURPRISING APPEARANCES...

THAT'S REALLY ORIGINAL!

A REAL EGGHEAD!

HELP ME CRACK THIS SHELL INSTEAD OF CRACKING UP!

HO HO HO HO HEH HEH HEH

AS FAR AS THE COLOR OF DINOSAURS GOES, WE CAN ONLY GUESS.

THIS COLOR'S GREAT FOR FLIRTING.

TOO GAUDY TO HIDE!

WHEN I TURN RED, YOU'D BETTER NOT COME LOOKING FOR ME!

YIKES!

SCRAW

SCRAW

RECENTLY, WE'VE FIGURED OUT THAT CERTAIN SPECIES, SUCH AS VELOCIRAPTORS, HAD FEATHERS...

YIPPEE! I'M THE KING OF THE WORLD!

BUT THEY WERE MORE FOR STAYING WARM THAN FOR FLYING.

WAAA FLOP

DURING THIS PERIOD, THE SEAS WERE ALSO FILLED WITH FEARSOME CREATURES SUCH AS THE GIGANTIC *LIOPLEURODON* HERE...

THAT'S BECAUSE I HAVE 80 FEET OF BODY TO FEED, KIDS!

AND WITH *PTEROSAURS*, THE SKIES WEREN'T LEFT EMPTY, EITHER.

FLY ME TO THE MOON-- LET ME PLAY AMONG THE STARS!

I WANT TO FLY AWAY FROM YOUR SONGS!

NOTE, HOWEVER, THAT LIOPLEURODON AND PTEROSAURS WERE MARINE AND FLYING REPTILES, AND NOT DINOSAURS!

DINOSAUR OR NOT, WHAT DIFFERENCE DOES IT MAKE?! I'LL BE GOBBLED UP EITHER WAY!

IT'S HARD, HARD, ≥AARGH≤ BEING A DINOSAUR!

BLOZ & PLUMERI

TROODON

LET'S GET TO KNOW THE *TROODON*...

OOH, LA, LA! WHAT DO I SEE?

A DINOSAUR THAT NOTICES EVERYTHING THAT ISN'T QUITE RIGHT...

WHATEVER ARE YOU DOING, TRICERATOPS!

? ? ?

BUT HIS MAIN CHARACTERISTIC IS INTELLIGENCE...

YOU'RE GOING TO BREAK YOUR HORNS AND THEY'RE YOUR ONLY WAY TO DEFEND YOURSELVES!

VERY INTELLIGENT...

AND YOU, THERE-- DO YOU WANT TO GET FOOD POISONING?

WHY ARE YOU EATING ROTTEN FERNS?

THERE ARE FRESH PLANTS RIGHT OVER THERE!

HMMM?

TAP TAP

CHROMPP GHRROARP GHRROTPP

AND HE LIKES TO MAKE THAT KNOWN...

?

IT'S NOT VERY SMART TO EAT HIM NOW, REX!

?

WAIT ANOTHER MONTH BEFORE NABBING HIM!

THAT WAY, HE'LL HAVE FATTENED UP NICELY AND YOU'LL HAVE TO CHASE HIM MUCH LESS!

BUT IN A WORLD OF BRUTES, IS THERE ROOM FOR BRAINS?

LEAVE US ALONE, NERD!

I'LL GET SNACKED ON WHEN I WANT!

YOU KNOW WHAT MY HORNS ARE TELLING YOU?

TROODON

MEANING: WOUNDING TOOTH
PERIOD: LATE CRETACEOUS (75-65 MILLION YEARS AGO)
ORDER/ FAMILY: SAURISCHIA/ TROODONTIDAE
SIZE: 6.5 FEET LONG
WEIGHT: 110 LBS.
DIET: CARNIVORE
FOUND: NORTH AMERICA

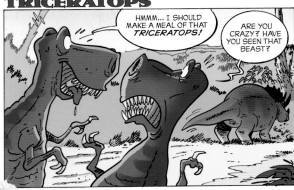

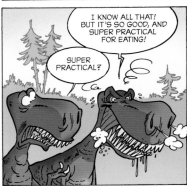

TRICERATOPS

MEANING: THREE-HORNED FACE
PERIOD: LATE CRETACEOUS (68-65 MILLION YEARS AGO)
ORDER/ FAMILY: ORNITHISCHIA/ CERATOPSIDAE
SIZE: 30 FEET LONG
WEIGHT: 20,000 LBS.
DIET: HERBIVORE
FOUND: NORTH AMERICA

FAMOUS DINOSAURS OF THE JURASSIC

THE FIRST DINOSAUR FROM THE JURASSIC TO BECOME FAMOUS WAS ALSO THE FIRST TO BE NAMED, IN 1824: *MEGALOSAURUS.*

I'M THE STRONGEST! I'M THE BEST!

WHAT A MEGALO-MANIAC!

ITS COUSIN, *ALLOSAURUS,* WAS A "MINIATURE" TYRANNOSAURUS REX-- BUT STILL 35 FEET LONG WITH 70 TEETH!

ROAR

YUCK! AND WHAT BAD BREATH, TOO!

CAMPTOSAURUS WAS LIKE A BIG COW THAT COULD DIGEST EVERY PLANT WITHIN REACH.

WHAT'RE YOU SAYING?

I SAID WE CAN'T HEAR EACH OTHER OVER THOSE DISGUSTING DIGESTION NOISES!

GROWL

GURGLE

AS FOR *STEGOSAURUS,* IT'S WELL KNOWN FOR ITS DORSAL PLATES AND SPIKED TAIL.

?

HEY, GUYS! ME, TOO! I'M WELL KNOWN!

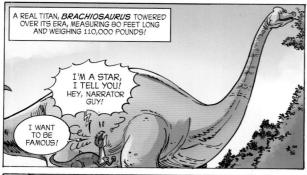

A REAL TITAN, *BRACHIOSAURUS* TOWERED OVER ITS ERA, MEASURING 80 FEET LONG AND WEIGHING 110,000 POUNDS!

I'M A STAR, I TELL YOU! HEY, NARRATOR GUY!

I WANT TO BE FAMOUS!

QUIET, SHRIMP!

SPLOTCH

!

HERE'S THE SKELETON OF A YOUNG COMPSOGNATHUS. ITS BONES WERE CRUSHED FOR SOME UNKNOWN REASON...

FLASH

FLASH

YAY! I'M FAMOUS!

MORE GREAT GRAPHIC NOVEL SERIES AVAILABLE FROM PAPERCUTZ

COMING SOON

SEA CREATURES #1

SEA CREATURES #2

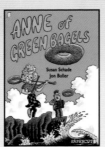

ANNE OF GREEN BAGELS #1

DISNEY FAIRIES #18

FUZZY BASEBALL

THE GARFIELD SHOW #6

THE LUNCH WITCH #1

DINOSAURS #1

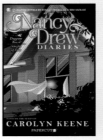

NANCY DREW DIARIES #7

THE RED SHOES

SCARLETT

THE SISTERS #1

THE WILD SMURF — THE SMURFS #21

GERONIMO STILTON #18

TROLLS #1

THE SMURFS, DISNEY FAIRIES, THE GARFIELD SHOW and TROLLS graphic novels are available for $7.99 in paperback, and $12.99 in hardcover. GERONIMO STILTON graphic novels are available for $9.99 in hardcover only. FUZZY BASEBALL and NANCY DREW DIARIES graphic novels are available for $9.99 in paperback only. SEA CREATURES and DINOSAURS graphic novels are available for $10.99 each in hardcover only. THE SISTERS graphic novels are available for $9.99 each in paperback, and $14.99 each in hardcover. THE LUNCH WITCH, SCARLETT, and ANNE OF GREEN BAGELS graphic novels are available for $14.99 in paperback only. THE RED SHOES graphic novel is available for $12.99 in hardcover only.
Available from booksellers everywhere. You can also order online from www.papercutz.com. Or call 1-800-886-1223, Monday through Friday, 9–5 EST. MC, Visa, and AmEx accepted. To order by mail, please add $4.00 for postage and handling for first book ordered, $1.00 for each additional book and make check payable to NBM Publishing.
Send to: Papercutz, 160 Broadway, Suite 700, East Wing, New York, NY 10038.

DINOSAURS, THE SISTERS, SEA CREATURES, THE SMURFS, THE GARFIELD SHOW, BARBIE, TROLLS, GERONIMO STILTON, FUZZY BASEBALL, THE LUNCH WITCH, NANCY DREW DIARIES, THE RED SHOES, ANNE OF GREEN BAGELS, and SCARLETT graphic novels are also available wherever e-books are sold.

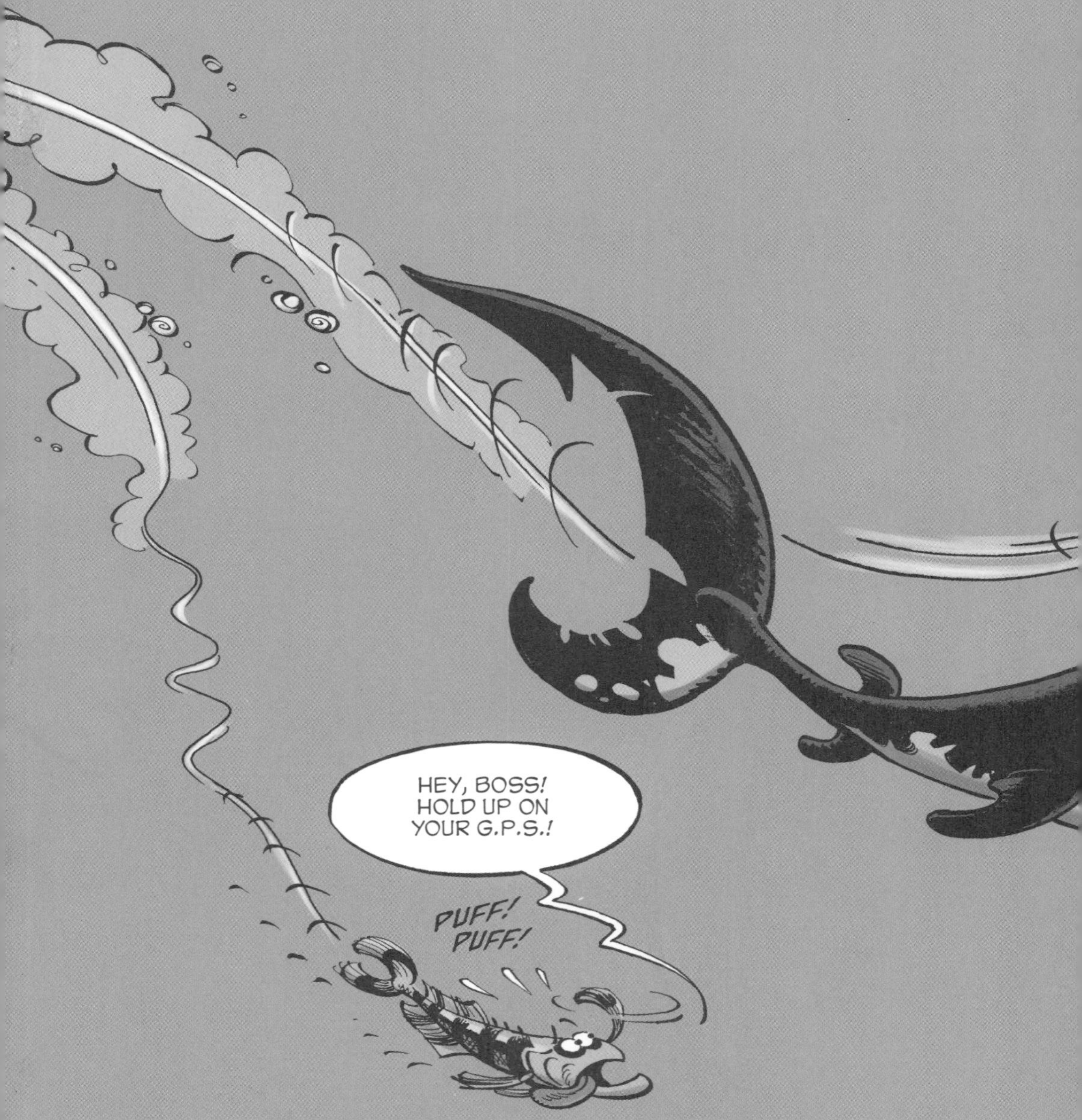
HEY, BOSS! HOLD UP ON YOUR G.P.S.!
PUFF! PUFF!